# Just Add Mistletoe

AN
**Everly Falls**
NOVEL

# Just Add Mistletoe

# HEATHER B. MOORE

Copyright © 2024 by Heather B. Moore
Print edition
All rights reserved

No part of this book may be reproduced in any form whatsoever without prior written permission of the publisher, except in the case of brief passages embodied in critical reviews and articles. This is a work of fiction. The characters, names, incidents, places, and dialogue are products of the author's imagination and are not to be construed as real.

Interior design by Cora Johnson
Edited by JL Editing Services and Lorie Humpherys
Cover design by Rachael Anderson
Cover image credit: Deposit Photos #229705576 NadianB
Published by Mirror Press, LLC
ISBN: 978-1-952611-46-9

## EVERLY FALLS SERIES
Just Add Romance
Just Add Mischief
Just Add Friendship
Just Add Mistletoe

## PINE VALLEY SERIES
Worth the Risk
Where I Belong
Say You Love Me
Waiting for You
Finding Us
Until We Kissed
Let's Begin Again
All For You

## PROSPERITY RANCH SERIES
One Summer Day
Steal My Heart
Not Over You
Seasoned with Love
Take a Chance

## HISTORICAL TITLES
The Paper Daughters of Chinatown
The Slow March of Light
In the Shadow of a Queen
Under the Java Moon
Condemn Me Not
Lady Flyer
Until Vienna
Love is Come

**Biblical Fiction under H.B. Moore**
Esther the Queen
Ruth
Eve: In the Beginning
The Moses Chronicles
Deborah: Prophetess of God
Mary and Martha
Hannah
Anna the Prophetess
Rebekah and Isaac

# Just Add Mistletoe

**She'll do anything to stay invisible to the male eye. But he can't seem to notice anyone else.**

Lori loves the holidays, and if her holiday store isn't a huge indicator, she dresses for each season. It makes her happy, and no man—so far—has been interested in her idiosyncrasies. But that doesn't matter since she's sworn off dating because of a series of flops. She's more than content, or at least that's what she thinks, until Malcom moves across the street from her. Literally. In a construction lot where he's taken up residence in a trailer.

Lori decides his housing choices are none of her business—but the two keep crossing paths and discover they have plenty in common. And all the things they are opposite in only add fuel to her attraction. Besides, he's not put off by her broomstick earrings, autumn leaf sweaters, or mistletoe hairbands. The only catch is that he's also sworn off dating. One of them will have to cave first.

# One

LORI HARDING'S FRIENDS WERE DROPPING like flies. Well, not like dead flies, but the type of dying off that came with husbands or even serious boyfriends. The dynamics of friendships changed. Weekends changed. Social lives changed. Or more accurately—died.

Lori hated labels, but she lived in a labeling world. So if she were to label herself, it would be a classic introvert. She didn't consider herself shy, but she was perfectly happy to have quiet nights at home, and she didn't mind much when social plans were canceled.

Until lately.

She could blame it on herself if she were to be perfectly honest, because *she* had in fact canceled the last two times on her friends. Saturday lunch, and then a few days later, they all caught a movie—with the exception of Julie, whose baby had been sick.

Lori's excuse? It was early October, which signaled the beginning of the busy holiday season for her small store, Holiday Express. And she was up to her neck in ordering and stocking.

Speaking of her friend group, a text buzzed her phone. Lori set down a box of Halloween decorations by the large front window. The shop was open already, but business was slow this morning.

Pulling out her phone from her pocket, Lori read Brandy's text: *Who's all in for the retreat? I need to send the deposit soon.*

Replies quickly came through from the other women in the group—all former high school classmates who somehow managed to stay friends more than ten years later.

*I'll talk to Austin tonight,* Everly wrote. *I'm sure one of our moms will be happy to watch Jessica. Or even both. Haha.*

Everly and Austin were newly married and completely devoted to each other. Jessica, Austin's seven-year-old daughter, rounded out the darling family.

*Perfect,* Brandy wrote.

Lori set her phone on the window ledge, then tugged off the tape from the box. She opened the cardboard flaps to see dozens of small plastic skeletons, forming a string of lights. She hoped they'd be as cute in the store window as they'd looked in the catalog. Her phone buzzed again, and she glanced at it.

*Dave and I are in,* Julie wrote. *My mom is going to stay here for the weekend. She'll be getting serious superwoman points.*

*Oh, she'll love it,* Everly replied. *Your kids are adorable.*

*Except when they're not,* Julie wrote, following with a winking emoji.

*We're in too,* Stephenie texted. *Our neighbor is going to keep an eye on Pops.*

*Yay!* Brandy wrote.

That situation had been up in the air for a couple of days. Stephenie and her boyfriend Cal were the caretakers of her step-grandfather. And now . . . they were down to one person who had yet to answer—Lori. She still hadn't committed even though she didn't have to consult with a boyfriend or husband,

and she didn't need to find a sitter for kids or someone to watch over a grandparent.

Nope. Lori was single, through and through. Her friends had bantered around the idea of her bringing a plus one—but since there was no plus one, the idea had fallen flat. The whole idea of a retreat sounded divine, if Lori were to say so herself. She rarely took more than a day off since opening her store, and even more rarely two days off.

Their small town of Everly Falls—yep, her friend shared the same name—wasn't exactly a hopping tourist destination, but it got its fair share of shopping during the holidays. Which meant that Lori couldn't do everything herself and had hired a part-timer, Marci—another former high school friend.

So Lori had dragged her feet on the retreat idea since she'd be the only one without a significant other coming. It just all felt . . . awkward. Not that her friends, or their boyfriends-slash-husbands, had ever made her feel that way. In fact, she liked the men and always enjoyed their times together when they did things as a group. But Lori would definitely be the odd one out. And if she brought that up, then Brandy would say her mom could come, or maybe one of their other single friends. But that would change up the dynamics once again—pulling them out of their close-knit circle of girlfriends.

And . . . here it came. The text from Brandy. *Lori—any update on scheduling Marci for the weekend?*

The text was innocent in its actual words, but the screen glowed mockingly at her.

Now was her chance to completely back out. She'd feel sad to miss it, though. Envious, mostly. But would she be more miserable missing it than if she went and was constantly surrounded by her friends snuggling up to their men?

Lori picked up the phone and stared at the text, weighing all the pros and cons in her mind. She didn't want to be a downer. If she didn't go, she'd forever hear about how much they'd "missed" her. If she did go, she'd have to stuff down all of her envious feelings where no one could draw them out.

If she didn't go, she'd get tons of work done at the shop, then spend more time at her parents' old house, getting it ready to put on the market by next spring. She'd agreed to do the work so they could move to Florida sooner. Besides, once the house sold, part of it would be her inheritance, bringing in money she sorely needed to expand the shop. Her parents had first told her she could live in the house, but she knew they were also counting on the proceeds from the sale to supplement their retirement. Besides, Lori really loved living right above her shop. She was thirty seconds from her work.

But . . . if she did go to the retreat, she wouldn't miss out on spending time with the people she loved most. The people who actually cared about her.

If she didn't go, she'd be able to forget how her dates seemed to cut off after two meetups, never getting to the third-date stage.

If she did go, then she'd maybe get out of her head a little bit. Hike some trails. She did love hiking, and she hadn't been all summer. Where had the time gone?

Maybe she could leave early if things became too much. She could come up with some work emergency—there was always work to do, and it might be an emergency to *her* . . . but that felt icky.

Lori closed her eyes, blew out a slow breath, then made up her mind. Opening her eyes, she typed a text to her part-time employee. *Are you good to cover the weekend if I go on that retreat?*

Marci's reply came seconds later. *Of course. Go enjoy yourself.*

Lori switched text threads: *Count me in. Marci can cover for the weekend.*

Heart emojis followed, and despite her wishy-washy self, Lori smiled. It would be fun—she'd make sure of it. She could certainly bury whatever emotions threatened to erupt. She didn't know what it was, but since she'd turned twenty-eight a few weeks ago, everything seemed different. Like she somehow needed to be more successful, more confident, more social, more involved—and even though she was a business owner, independent, a good person, she was somehow lacking. She spent way too much time feeling lonely.

Yes, she'd always been alone in a sense, but she'd never felt lonely.

And it bothered her. Not that she was alone—she'd never force a relationship or become desperate for one—but because she didn't like having feelings she didn't want to have.

Brandy, efficient as always, sent out the payment breakdown and Lori quickly sent in her share. There. She could put this whole retreat thing on the back burner. She dug into the box again and pulled out a plastic cauldron. She planned to keep it smoking with dry ice. That would fascinate the kids. The teenagers too.

The front door swung open, the bell tinkling overhead.

"Oh, it's crazy out there," Marci said, unwrapping one of two scarves about her neck.

It might be October, but it was hardly scarf-wearing weather yet. That didn't seem to deter Marci. She celebrated the changing seasons as if it were an Olympic sport. Her enthusiasm was one of the reasons Lori had hired her. Also, it was kind of ironic that popular high school cheerleader Marci now worked for the geeky, introverted Lori.

"Crazy? How?" Lori peered out the front window. The morning sky was a soft blue. No rain clouds. It wasn't even windy.

Then she saw it. Across the street, where the old auto shop used to be, a group of people had gathered, picket signs in hand. It was a bit comical, in Lori's point of view, to protest against a development the city council had already approved. The town citizen input for the building project was several months ago. What made today so special?

Marci answered the unasked question.

"Today they break ground. Look, the ones with the signs are against the development, and the ones wearing construction vests are in favor of the development. I guess they bought out all the bright orange fabric at the craft store last night. Must have been up all night sewing." She came to stand by Lori, twisting off the top of her diet soda bottle.

There'd been a massive sign erected in the corner of the property stating *Millpond Condos* in bold black and green for months, so it was no secret that the developmental project had been approved by the city council.

"Is that Lydia Kane?" she asked, eyeing the woman who was Everly and Brandy's mom. Lydia wore a linen suit, her hair and makeup impeccable as always. She held a sign high in the air that read in boxy red letters: *Say No To The Big Man.*

"Sure is," Marci said, her tone light. "Want to join in? Could be fun. Heard the café is delivering sandwiches and drinks soon."

Unlike Marci, Lori had eaten breakfast, and besides, she wasn't opposed to the building of a condominium community. Not that she shared the opinion with her store customers. She figured that not only would it bring more business to her store, but it would give the young adults growing up in the town a place to live. Otherwise, they just all moved out and on with their lives.

"Oh boy," Marci muttered at the precise moment Lori saw a couple of trucks turn onto the street, followed by a flatbed carrying an excavator. "It's happening now. Should I pop some popcorn? Get out some chairs?"

Lori laughed. They didn't have any popcorn even if they wanted some. "The protestors look pretty harmless. Besides, I really want to get all of these boxes unpacked today."

Lori liked Marci a lot—they'd definitely become friends over the past two years—but sometimes she needed reminding that she was on the clock.

"Right, boss." Marci downed a couple of swallows of her diet soda, then set it on the windowsill. She pulled out the last of what was in the box—a couple of light-up jack-o-lanterns—then began to open the next one.

Lori relocated the soda bottle to a safer location, then carried over the stool and began to hang the strand of skeleton lights. The trucks had now slowed and were turning onto the property.

The gaggle of protesters crowded around the first truck, raising their signs and chanting something—it was muffled through the window. Lori was a bit impressed. Lydia Kane and her friends were going all out.

The truck came to a rolling stop, and a man jumped out and walked around, then headed straight for the gathered protesters.

"You've gotta give that man credit," Marci said, popping up again and startling her. "He's not afraid of confrontation."

"Is that the property owner?" Lori asked. From this distance, about all she could see was a red ball cap and broad shoulders. He was tall—she'd give him that.

"Yeah, that's him," Marci said. "My husband went to all those council meetings. The guy is from out of town, of course, so that always gets everyone's backs up."

The man was currently holding up a hand as if asking for everyone to quiet down. The drivers of the other trucks climbed out, wearing construction vests. The crowd seemed to grow—had more people arrived? Lori estimated at least fifty people . . . amazing that so many would gather in this sleepy town.

She tore her gaze away and continued with stringing the lights.

"Oh my gosh!" Marci said.

Lori looked at her, then out the window. A fight had broken out between the two groups. She wasn't quite sure what had happened. But people were throwing punches and women were pulling at other women, and someone screamed.

Lori was so stunned, she couldn't move for a moment, then she jumped off the stool and hurried to the front door. She didn't have a plan, but she wanted to get Lydia Kane out of the fray. She hurried across the street toward the chaos, her heart thumping. Lydia wasn't too hard to pick out because she stood on the edge of the crowd, her hand to her chest as if she couldn't believe what she was seeing.

"Mrs. Kane," Lori called out. "Come with me. Let's get you out of this mayhem."

"Lori?" Lydia's eyes widened when she spotted her. "Can you believe all of this?"

Just then, sirens sounded, and that seemed to break up the crowd. A few people headed off down the street. Two women were in a shouting match. A man on the anti-development side cradled his nose, which was dripping with blood.

"Come on," Lori said again, clasping Mrs. Kane's arm. "It sounds like the cops are on their way to sort everything out. Let's just head into my shop to stay out of the way."

Lydia looked reluctant to leave, but Lori wasn't having any of it. "Lydia," she said in a firm tone. "I think it's better we get out of the way."

Finally, the woman nodded and turned. They crossed the street to where Marci stood at the door, holding it open. "Are you all right, Mrs. Kane?" she asked.

"Oh, I'm fine," Lydia said. "This whole town has gone mad. This was supposed to be a peaceful protest."

"Have a seat here," Lori said, motioning to one of the armchairs she kept by the fireplace that made a cozy nook during the winter months. She pulled out her phone and sent a quick text to Brandy and Everly, telling them that their mom was fine, but she'd been part of an incident.

Brandy replied immediately, saying she was on her way.

"Oh boy," Marci murmured.

Lori looked up to see someone approaching their shop. A tall man with a red ball cap. He tugged open the door.

Lydia yelped. "It's the devil himself!"

The man's frame seemed to fill the whole door, and Lori found herself staring into a pair of hazel eyes that seemed to bore right into her. The man was handsome, she'd give him that. If, that was, someone found an angular-jaw-dark-lashes-hazel-eyes look attractive.

No one in the shop spoke. Likely because they were all staring at him.

"Do you happen to have any ice?" he asked, taking another step closer in his construction boots. "A man out there has a broken nose."

# Two

MALCOM GRAVES HAD NEVER MADE three women speechless before. But that was happening at this moment. The fifty-something lady in the chair looked like she wanted to murder him, the redhead grinned from ear to ear, and the brunette stared at him with blue eyes that might technically be considered black.

He tried again. "Sorry to intrude, but do you happen to have ice?" He glanced around—what was this place? It smelled like someone had thrown a potpourri of flowers into a simmering pot. As far as he could see, there were knickknacks everywhere—like the things that you found at a garage sale.

"Don't let him in," the older woman said, her sugary voice belying her stern words.

"We don't have any ice," the redhead announced. "Try at the end of the block. There's a grocery store there."

"That will take too long," the brunette said. Her dark hair was pulled into a sleek ponytail. Silver earrings dangled from her ears—were those . . . cat earrings? She wore all black—black jeans, black V-neck shirt, and short black boots. She moved past the redhead. "I'll get a cold washcloth for him." She stopped in front of a shelf that read *Back to School* and grabbed what looked like a hand towel with the same message.

Then she continued toward a narrow hallway.

"Oh, and you can come in," she called over her shoulder. "Probably safer inside."

Malcom hesitated because the older woman's glare was quite fierce. It wasn't like he was looking for a safe place—the protesters wouldn't hurt him. He was pretty sure the man with the broken nose was an unintentional injury. But what did he really know? This small, cozy town of Everly Falls was turning out not to be so cozy after all.

"Here you are." The brunette was back.

What color were her eyes? And was that a freckle next to her ear? One freckle only? The rest of her skin was freckle free.

She pressed the cold, wet towel into his hands, because apparently he was staring at her. Somehow he managed to pull himself out of whatever rabbit hole he'd fallen into. "Thanks, miss."

"It's Lori. I'm not really a *miss*, but thanks for not calling me a *ma'am*."

*Lori*. Easy enough to remember. "I'm Malcom Grave—"

"We know who you are," the older woman said from her chair perch.

That was his cue. "Thanks again." He lifted the towel. "I'll return it." Pause. "After I clean it, of course."

He turned to leave, wondering if this day could get any stranger. It was only eight thirty in the morning, so he supposed it was entirely possible.

"I'll come help," the woman, Lori, said. "Can you watch the store, Marci? Oh, and Mrs. Kane, Brandy is on her way."

That was a lot of names, but Malcom was pretty good with names. Regardless, his first instinct was to tell Lori not to worry about it. She probably didn't want to be in the thick of whatever was happening now. At least the cops had arrived, and the crowd was mostly dispersed.

The protesting didn't bother Malcolm too much. It had happened a handful of times in the past several years—and if history repeated itself, the residents who were up in arms would calm over a few days' time, and eventually, the quiet town would become quiet again.

Ironically, in this situation, he'd been approached by the city council. Some other hotshot developer had tried to bulldoze their way into Everly Falls with a massive renovation plan. The council had been wary, and although they conceded there needed to be adequate housing for the growing town, they weren't ready to take ten leaps forward. A single step was just fine, and thus, Malcom had come into the picture.

One of the deals was that he couldn't divulge that he'd been contacted first. The city council had a reputation to protect. And Malcom was more than happy for the business. It seemed condominium jobs were all going to the major construction companies. He ran a small company with his stepbrother, and it had been great for the most part. But after this Everly Falls project, he wanted to look for a more permanent residence and focus on building single-family homes or renovations.

What his brother would choose to do, Malcom didn't know. He was more of a number-crunching guy, while Malcom was the guy in front of the city councils and residents, buttering them up and shaking hands.

"Excuse me," he said, approaching the group huddled around the man with a broken nose, sitting on the sidewalk curb, hand on his face, blood between his fingers. "I've got a wet cloth that will help."

He felt the glares thrown at him, rather than actually seeing them, because he was focused on the sixty-something-year-old man.

Malcom sat on the curb next to him. "Here, let's press this against your face."

"Mr. Ronning," Lori said, settling on the other side of the man. "Are you all right?"

Mr. Ronning lowered his hand slowly and accepted the wet towel. She helped him adjust it. "I'm okay," he said in a muffled voice.

"What happened?" Lori asked.

"Got an elbow in the face from Bernice," he said. "Was an accident, that's all. I told as much to the cops."

"Well, I'm sorry about that," Lori said in a soothing tone. "So none of the construction workers harmed you?"

"No," he said.

"And this man's in the clear?" she asked, motioning toward Malcom.

Mr. Ronning gave a subtle nod. "Yep. And don't worry, I don't need to see any doctor. One of the cops already checked it out—used to be a paramedic." His gaze zeroed in on Malcom. "But stirring things up is never good, sir."

Malcom's skin pricked with heat. The day would be a warm one, and the morning coolness was fading fast. "I went through all the proper channels and received all the permissions. Grievances were heard and addressed last month."

Mr. Ronning didn't look pleased at his comeback, but it was Lori's expression he was more interested in. Was that a glimmer of a smile on her face? Her dark hair had caught the sun's rays, giving it some bronzed highlights. Blue, he decided. Her eyes were definitely blue. The brightening sky behind her confirmed it.

Malcom couldn't afford to be distracted right now. He had a protest to disperse, a city council to keep happy, and the first day of construction to start. Every hour was money, in his book. And every wasted hour, even more expensive.

Which reminded him. He had to get Mr. Ronning situated so he could do his job. "If you need anything, I'm happy to help, Mr. Ronning," Malcom said. "Provided it doesn't disrupt the building project."

The man didn't laugh.

"Do you need a ride home?" he continued. "Can I bring you a drink? I hear there's a grocery store at the end of the street."

Mr. Ronning waved a hand. "I'm fine. My wife's already on her way to pick me up."

"I've got him," Lori told Malcom.

"Do you want to sit in my shop?" she asked Mr. Ronning. "It's more comfortable than this cement curb."

It took Mr. Ronning only a half second to agree, and Malcom was left standing on the curb, watching the two cross the street—Mr. Ronning's walk more of a shuffle, Lori's silver cat earrings catching the light. He kept his gaze firmly on her swaying ponytail and not her swaying hips as questions rushed through his mind. What was Lori's last name? Was she involved with anyone? She wasn't wearing a wedding ring—but not everyone wore a ring. Would she have joined the protesters if she didn't have a shop to run? He adjusted his ball cap, then rubbed his neck. Focus, he told himself.

Then he crossed to the cops, who were now talking to his construction crew. "Everything good?" he asked.

"Everything's fine now," one of the officers said. "The mayor is arriving at any moment to talk to the residents. Give you his support. But you're free to move your excavator and start working."

Relief rushed through Malcom. When all was said and done, the delay had been less than an hour.

The crew broke up, climbed back into the trucks, and the procession moved forward. Malcom hopped in his own truck, found a place to park, and climbed out just as a pink truck pulled into the lot.

His heart sank.

Penny Gilchrist stepped out, dressed like a cross between a Barbie Instagram influencer and a Halloween costume of a construction worker. He wanted to laugh, but he couldn't. Penny was his sister-in-law's sister, although the two women couldn't be more different. Kari was completely down to earth, and Penny . . . well, she floated above the earth on most days.

"Malc!" Penny said in her singsong tone. She was thirty-four, two years older than him, and had definitely been through some living, most of which she covered up with layers of makeup. "Happy first day!"

She swung her hip against the truck door since her hands were full of what looked like coffee and a sack of pastries or bagels.

Malcom knew he couldn't totally avoid her since she worked for the company as their operations manager. The woman was as smart as a whip, which only made him more wary. He always felt like she was setting traps around him, and he invariably stepped in every single one. He'd once confessed to his brother how uncomfortable he was with Penny's overt friendliness, but Bronson had just laughed. Told him he was overreacting. Told him that was just Penny's personality. It would be too weird if she crushed on him.

Oh, Malcom agreed with that, but how else would anyone define it? The generous gifts, the leading questions, the affectionate touches, the laughter when he hadn't said anything funny at all.

As she neared, he tried not to wince at the sight of Penny practically teetering as she walked on high heels. Who wore high heels to a construction site? Penny Gilchrist, apparently.

"You're looking fine, Malc," she gushed, her smile wide, face framed by wavy blonde hair.

He tamped down his irritation at the way she shortened

his name to Malc. He'd been called Mac plenty of times—that, he didn't mind—but *Malc?* Sounded like some sort of foot powder.

Penny's all-pink ensemble stood out like a flashing light in the middle of a foggy night. "I love your construction-boy look. Very handsome."

Malcom forced his expression to remain nonplussed. He was wearing the most basic outfit. Gray T-shirt, jeans, construction boots. A ball cap.

"What brings you all the way out here?" he asked, because he was truly curious. They all worked out of their homes, and Penny lived about a thirty-minute drive from Everly Falls.

"Just making a special delivery." She held up the sack. "Apple tarts. Your favorite."

Malcom had no idea where she got that idea from. Sure, he liked apple tarts. He liked all food, in fact. But he wasn't much of a breakfast person. So something like apple tarts sounded way too sweet.

He took the sack because she was practically shoving it into his face. "Well, thank you. I'm sure I'll enjoy them at some point today."

Penny laughed. Then she inched closer. "Did you see all those protestors? Do you think this will be on the news?"

Malcom set the sack inside the bed of his truck. "I doubt it," he said, shoving his hands in his pockets and stepping away from her. "I don't see any journalists or cameras."

"Oh right." Penny laughed again. "Hey, before you talk to the workers, or whatever it is you do, I need your advice."

He would have preferred to walk away, but she grasped his arm, her long fingernails like talons against his skin.

"I went to a dance club last night with my girlfriends, and this guy kept hitting on me." She pushed her lips into a pout. "I mean he was cute, but kind of young for me. Maybe in his mid-twenties. I didn't want to be rude, so I took his number. But now I'm wondering if I should have just said no and told him about *you*."

Malcom stared at her. What was she saying? What did she mean? "And . . . what would you have told a complete stranger at a bar about *me*?"

"Oh, you know, that I have a really cool boss and he's the jealous type." She winked at him as her hand slid up his arm.

Malcom was at an even greater loss now. "What exactly would I be jealous of?"

Penny laughed. "Oh, you know." Her phone rang just then, and she released his arm and pulled out the phone from her pocket. She glanced at the caller ID. "It's that homeowners' association that I'm trying to secure a maintenance contract with." Before Malcom could question her about it, she answered, "Hello?"

He remembered his brother saying that Penny was looking into setting up maintenance accounts with an affluent cabin complex in the canyon above Everly Falls. Malcom had been against it. Starting this condominium project would stretch everyone thin as it was. Apparently, it was already in the works, and Malcom had no say. Which was kind of par for the course over the past year since Penny had joined the company. Another reason he wanted to do his own thing.

With Penny distracted, Malcom headed toward the job site. He sincerely hoped she wouldn't stick around and that they wouldn't have to continue the conversation she'd started. He had his own phone calls to make. Primarily to find out when the trailer would be delivered. It would be his temporary home and office for the next few months.

He told himself to ignore the fact that camping out on the property that was right across from the holiday shop would give him plenty of chances to cross paths with Lori.

# Three

Lori finished packing on Friday afternoon, adding a swimsuit at the last minute. Brandy had said the cabin had a hot tub, although she didn't plan to get into it if it became a couples thing. She grabbed three books from her to-be-read pile on her bedside table. Maybe she'd get some reading time, maybe not. But she wanted to be prepared.

She glanced about her apartment on the upper level of the shop. Had she forgotten anything? Her gaze paused on the cat bed in the corner of the bedroom. She hadn't thrown it out even though it had been a couple of months since her cat's death. Lori knew Silver wasn't coming back, but just having the bed still in her room made her feel less abandoned somehow.

Lori's phone buzzed with a text announcing that Brandy and Ian were there to pick her up. They were a beautiful couple and fun to be around. They'd gotten engaged last month, right after Everly and Austin's wedding. Ian owned a gorgeous cabin in a secluded area just above Everly Falls, and he had turned his furniture-building hobby into a career.

Lori headed down the narrow stairs, then paused inside the shop to say goodbye to Marci. She looked up from where she was arranging a Halloween candy display. "Have so much fun! And don't worry about a thing."

"Thanks so much," Lori said, flashing a smile, then headed toward the front door of the shop. She had only one duffle bag—she'd packed light with the exception of her books.

Ian climbed out of the driver's seat as she exited the shop. The guy looked like he was ready to walk into the forest and chop more wood for his custom furniture business. His olive skin was set off by a red plaid shirt, and his light green eyes turned up at the corners as he smiled at her. "How are you, Lori?"

"Great, thanks."

Ian opened the back door for her and then took her bag to set in the trunk of the car. Brandy rolled down her window, her pale blonde hair tugging in the breeze.

"Hey, lady, so glad you could come."

"Me too." Lori climbed into the back seat and relaxed against the leather upholstery. "Where is this place again?"

"Oh, it's not far," Brandy said. "Didn't you open the link I sent? It's just above Everly Falls, where all those cabins are going in."

"Oh right." It sounded vaguely familiar, and Lori pulled up the texting thread and began to scroll back. Now that she was in the moment and had time to focus, she'd look at the details of the cabin.

"They've made tons of progress already," Ian said as they drove past the condominium construction site.

Lori looked over at the trucks and heavy-duty machinery, all working from sunup to sundown. There was a trailer parked on the lot too, and crew men all over the place. Marci had been giving her reports on the progress, although she hadn't been paying too much attention.

"There are still protesters?" Brandy said with a laugh. "Not even my mom is that hardcore."

"It looks more like coffee hour to me," Lori mused. About

a half a dozen people were camped out on the corner of the lot—chairs set up and coffee cups in hand. After the initial incident a few days ago, she hadn't given the protesters much thought. She might have thought of the foreman, Malcom, a time or two. Was he a foreman? Was that what he was called? She knew little to nothing about construction job titles.

"Malcom Graves seems like a decent guy," Ian said. "I've talked to him at the gym a few times. I don't get why some people are up in arms about the project."

Wait . . . Malcom Graves went to the town gym? Did he *live* in Everly Falls? Lori was curious now. Maybe not enough to question Ian further, yet how else would she find out?

"Don't let my mom hear you say that," Brandy said with a laugh. "I'm surprised she's not still keeping vigil with the protestors."

"Believe me, I'm keeping silent on the subject." He reached for Brandy's hand and the two interlaced their fingers.

Lori smiled to herself. She was really happy for Brandy and Ian, especially after what she had endured with her former boyfriend. Ian had appeared in Brandy's life just when she needed him most.

Lori shook off the melancholy that threatened as she wondered what her future relationships might be like—if any. Yeah, Everly Falls was a small town, but it was certainly growing. She glanced out the back window at the construction site they'd already passed. The progress was pretty incredible. Holes had been dug, cement foundations poured, and steel beams were going up.

Maybe she should invest in a condo. The apartment above the shop was so small—and she'd thought once or twice that it might make a cool reading nook for customers. But people probably wouldn't want to trudge up and down the stairs. So she'd been looking into the vacant space next door—it used to be an insurance office. If she bought it, she could expand her shop and have the new space as a bookshop.

But that would all be dependent on how much her parents' house sold for and what cut they gave her. Lori had no idea of what that might actually look like.

Her thoughts returned to the present as they headed up the canyon. The drive was beautiful, with the autumn colors growing richer and richer the farther they drove. They passed the turnoff for the trail to the waterfalls and continued up the windy road.

Lori had driven through a couple of the cabin community neighborhoods when they were first being built a couple of years ago. But she hadn't been up this far since. Now, the sight blew her away.

"Wow. This is amazing." She peered out the window at the impeccably landscaped properties and the elegant cabins. "Who owns these places? They must cost millions of dollars."

"From what I hear, they're owned by corporations," Brandy said. "Used for retreats and conferences."

When Ian turned into one of the properties, Lori was still staring. "Is that a pond? And a . . . zipline?"

Brandy laughed. "You still haven't looked at the link I sent, have you?"

"No." It was too late now. She'd just see everything in person.

Two cars were already in the massive circular driveway.

"Looks like we're the last ones here. Everly and Austin drove with Steph and Cal. Julie and Dave brought their own car in case they have to get back for anything with the kids."

Lori's heart lifted as she climbed out of the car and was greeted with fresh air that smelled of pine and rich earth. She'd forgotten how invigorating it could be in the canyon.

She decided that she'd love being around everyone, even

if she was the only one going solo. She was glad she'd come after all.

The front door opened, and Everly and Steph came outside. Everly's dark blonde hair was a mass of curls, barely contained with an oversized clip. She wore off-white jeans with decorative patches and a long-sleeved orange shirt. Steph's auburn hair had been curled and styled—different than her usual messy bun or ponytail she wore to her job as a hairdresser. She, of course, wore a dress—her signature style. This dress was loose knit and a deep green color.

"You made it!" Everly said. Everyone hugged, even though they saw each other plenty.

"Come on," Steph said. "I'll give you the grand tour. Ian, you'll find the guys in the great room trying to figure out how to work the fireplace. It's supposed to get pretty cold tonight."

Julie came out of the cabin just then and hugged Lori. "I feel so free," she gushed. "No kids. I don't know what to do with myself."

Lori laughed. "You'll get used to it soon enough and not want to go back."

Julie grinned. "Maybe. Except I've already texted my mom-in-law for any updates."

They walked with Steph around the cabin, assigning bedrooms, and then looking through the food items Steph had said she'd be in charge of. "I don't want us to have to go into town for any meals. We'll prepare everything here, and it will all be easy."

"How long did this take you to put together?" Lori asked, looking in the well-stocked fridge.

"Oh, I ordered it all online and then Cal and I loaded it up on our way." Steph opened a bag of chocolate candy and poured it into a huge bowl. "Couldn't forget the chocolate though."

As Lori snagged a couple of pieces, she heard, "The hot tub's not warming up," coming from one of the men.

Everyone headed out on the back deck, which was huge and looked out on a gorgeous vista of pine trees intermingled with aspens.

Austin was crouched before the hot tub controllers, but nothing was happening. The water jets wouldn't even turn on. When he stood, Brandy said, "I'll call the owner. This was part of the package, and it should work."

She headed into the cabin while Lori and Julie dragged a couple of chairs toward the edge of the deck. They sat in the shade as the sound of aspen leaves rustled in the wind.

"Someone will be here in an hour or two," Brandy announced from the sliding door. "So we'll hot tub after dinner."

After that, everyone kind of scattered. Brandy and Ian went on a nature hike. Everly and Austin were on dinner duty and began preparations.

Dave came out to sit with Julie and Lori, and they ended up talking about the condominium project. "It's just a slippery slope," he said. "This gets approved, and what's next? An amusement park? A zoo? Another condo project? Pretty soon Everly Falls will be crawling with people, and we'll have to expand the roads."

Lori listened absently, wondering if it would be rude to escape to her room and read until dinner.

Steph and Cal came outside, and he fiddled with the hot tub settings again, but no luck.

Finally, Lori went inside to help with dinner, and by the time Brandy and Ian returned, the chicken tortilla soup was ready, along with several sides. Darkness fell outside, and still no maintenance person showed up.

Brandy made another phone call, then hung up, her

expression worried. "I guess there's a new company that's handling things, and they just started yesterday. So there's been a delay on some of the jobs."

Julie waved a hand. "Let's play board games. Dave brought like five of them."

Playing games ended up being a lot of fun, and the time flew by. Around eleven o'clock, a few people headed to their rooms, leaving Lori, Brandy, and Ian downstairs by the fire. It had grown cold, and the fire also kept things cheery.

When a knock sounded on the door, Lori nearly jumped out of her seat.

"Probably the hot tub guy," Brandy said with a laugh as Ian unfolded himself from the couch.

"Unless someone ordered a late-night dessert," he said, throwing a questioning look at Brandy.

"I made no orders."

Ian crossed to the front door and opened it. By the muffled conversation, Lori knew it was another man. Then she heard the words "hot tub" and glanced over at Brandy, who was smiling.

"Finally," she whispered. "Hope it's an easy fix."

Lori turned when Ian walked into the great room with another man, a smile on his face. "Look who's on call tonight," he said. "This is Malcom Graves."

He wasn't wearing a ball cap, but Lori would have recognized him anyway. In fact, he was dressed in a button-down shirt, slacks, and leather shoes—as if he'd been at some other event. Maybe even on a date? His eyes were hooded in the low light of the cabin, his expression stoic.

"Oh." Brandy pushed to her feet. "Are you really the repair guy? I thought you owned a construction company."

Malcom's gaze moved from Brandy to Lori. If he recognized her, he didn't give any indication. "I do, and apparently, we're newly contracted for the maintenance of this community, but our operations manager neglected to inform the association that our crew is already dipping into overtime. It looks like I'm the man on call this weekend until I can get someone hired on Monday. Anyone here looking for a job?"

Ian laughed. "I've got my own job, thanks."

"Figures," Malcom deadpanned. "Well, lead the way." He picked up a tool bag that sat at his feet.

Lori rose from her chair as Brandy and Ian followed him through the cabin to the back deck. She trailed after them, kind of feeling sorry that Malcom came all this way to do something that he probably would hire out himself. Where did he live anyway? How far had he driven?

By the time she arrived on the back deck, Malcom had a panel open, and Ian was holding up a flashlight. Lori joined Brandy where she was leaning against the rail.

"He's cute," Brandy whispered as she nudged Lori's arm. "Want me to ask if he's single?"

"In what universe would I ever want you to ask that?" she scoffed. "We're not in elementary school anymore."

Brandy laughed, catching Ian's attention, which meant he walked over to them. "You ladies want to hot tub tonight? Looks like it will be fixed soon."

Lori allowed herself another glance at Malcom. He had a couple of tools out and was working away.

"I'd love to," Brandy told Ian, her voice soft, hand slipping into his.

Oh no, Lori wasn't going to join their love boat. "I'm getting pretty tired, so I'll probably head to bed soon."

The lights inside the hot tub came on. A very good sign. Next, the jets started up.

"Great, man," Ian said. "Thanks so much."

"No problem." Malcom packed up his tools, then straightened to face them. "You folks have a good night."

"Wait," Ian said, releasing Brandy's hand and stepping forward. "Do you want a drink or something? If you're hungry, we have tons of leftover dinner."

Malcom paused. "Water would be great. I sort of left in the middle of something to hurry up here."

"Something important?" Brandy asked. "I feel so bad."

"Oh, it wasn't important, exactly," he said. "It was . . . a relief. I was on a blind date, actually, a double date. And I'm pretty sure the woman who was supposed to be my date would have much rather been paired with my friend."

# Four

MALCOM WONDERED WHY HE'D GONE and said he'd been on a blind date. While it was true, it was kind of embarrassing to admit. He was thirty-two years old, and surely by now, he could manage his own dating life. So what if it had been lacking for a while? Although that was probably why his buddy Jay had set him up. The date had been with Jay and his girlfriend Kathleen, and Kathleen's best friend Leesa. Apparently Leesa didn't get the memo about not crushing on her best friend's man because the woman couldn't take her eyes off Jay all night.

Should Malcom say something? Had he imagined everything? Whatever was actually going on, he had been annoyed at the interruption of frantic texts from Penny, until he realized it would get him out of the nearly three-hour date.

It might be after eleven p.m. now, but he was far from tired. Besides, Ian was a cool guy—about the only person who'd been friendly at the gym. But Malcom wasn't fooling himself. The only reason he agreed to accept a drink and then a bowl of chicken tortilla soup was because he was intrigued by Lori. Not that he was thinking of asking her out—she might have a boyfriend—but because he could tell there was a lot going on behind those blue eyes of hers. For some reason, she'd hardly spoken a word. And it made him curious.

In his line of work, the women he was around were outspoken and shared their opinions readily. Lori seemed the opposite. Did she own that shop, or did she just work there? Why was she wearing cat earrings again? These ones were small black cats perched on tiny brooms. Was she the proverbial cat woman? Or a Halloween enthusiast? She wore all black again—a black sweatshirt and leggings.

"This is really good," Malcom said, because he felt like everyone in the kitchen was watching him eat.

Lori sat at the other end of the island. Brandy and Ian were leaning against each other, arms around one another, looking cozy. Maybe Lori didn't have a boyfriend—otherwise wouldn't he be here? Hanging out?

"How have you liked Everly Falls?" Ian asked. "I mean, after the protest on your first excavation day?"

Malcom wiped his mouth with a napkin. "It's been quiet for the most part. I mean, the protestors are still camping out—which is a bit strange. Maybe they're professional protestors and go from town to town?"

Ian laughed, and Malcom caught a smile on Lori's face. For some reason, that made him pleased.

"That would be truly wild," Brandy said. "Except I know the names of each and every one. At least my mom gave up after the first day."

Malcom felt like he'd swallowed a rock. "Oh, I'm sorry—will your mom be mad you're talking to me?"

Brandy grinned and shrugged. "No one has to know."

Malcom glanced over at Lori. "Was that the woman who called me a devil in your shop?'

Brandy gasped. "She *did*?"

Lori's smile appeared. She had those straight teeth that

had to be either from braces or perfect genetics. "She did. I think Brandy's right. No one has to know about you being here."

Malcom chuckled. "All right. Fair enough. Trying to keep family relations happy. I get it." He looked back to Ian. "Does one of you own this place?"

"No, we're just renting it for the weekend," Ian said. "A bunch of us are here—the rest have already gone to bed."

"Yeah, my sister and her husband are here," Brandy added. "Also, Julie and her husband Dave. Plus our high school friend Stephenie and her boyfriend. I guess he went to high school with us too—although it was only for a short time . . ."

Brandy continued to rattle on about Cal Conner and his speckled past with his parents—was that something the guy wanted to be public? And as interesting and entertaining as Brandy might be, Malcom kind of wanted to just talk to Lori. She was definitely looking at him plenty—not that he was reading anything into it. In all the people Brandy had listed, it seemed there wasn't anyone paired up with Lori.

When Brandy ran out of her rundown on the others staying in the house, Malcom said, "Oh, so you were all high school friends? Grew up in Everly Falls together?"

"Yeah," she confirmed. "It's kind of amazing we're all still here and we're all still best friends."

"That is amazing," he said. "I haven't kept in touch with any of my high school friends. I wouldn't even go to a reunion if they had one."

"Bad high school experience?" Lori asked.

Malcom hesitated, mostly because Lori was the one who asked the question. He'd finished his soup, so he rose and crossed to the sink to wash out the bowl. "I was a transfer, and everyone hated me from the beginning."

"What? Why?" Brandy asked.

Malcom turned from the sink and folded his arms. "I moved in with my dad and stepbrother after my mom remarried and moved to Costa Rica. Bronson's parents had been divorced for a while, and his dad was still in the picture, so I was definitely the odd man out most of the time. I focused on sports most of the time. Bronson and I are the same age, and we were competitive, to say the least. When I became the starter on the basketball team, playing over him, he was upset. Understandably. But when football started, I was picked as starting receiver, and my brother didn't talk to me for a month."

"You played both sports?" Lori asked.

Malcom met her blue gaze. "Small town—we played every sport."

The edges of her mouth quirked. "Oh, so you know how small towns are steeped in tradition?"

"I do." He shrugged. "Bronson forgave me when we won the regional title, then state title."

"In football?" Ian asked.

"Both football and basketball."

"Nice." Ian fist-bumped him. "Did you play in college?"

"I did, and so did Bronson. Basketball for a division two. I think that's what put us on good terms again. I mean, we own a company together now."

"Oh, that's cool," Ian said. "Do you and your brother live around here?"

Malcom grimaced. "Uh, no. My brother and his wife are about an hour north. I live . . . wherever the job is."

"Like you rent a place in each town?" Ian asked.

"Not exactly," he hedged. "I live in the trailer on the job lot. Doubles as an office too."

"You live in the *trailer*?" Brandy asked.

"The one across the street from my shop?" Lori added.

So it was her shop; he'd been wondering about that.

"Wow, that's impressive," Ian said. "Nothing gets by you at the job site, I'm guessing."

Malcom cracked a smile at this. "Not much."

But both Brandy and Lori were staring at him like he'd just confessed he was born on the moon.

"What are you, like a workaholic?" Brandy asked, her voice filled with disbelief.

"That's one way to look at it." Malcom felt a bit put on the spot. He was fine with the get-to-know-you questions, but now he felt called out.

"So . . ." Ian drawled. "When you go on a date, there's no 'hey, let's go back to my place and hang out.'"

Brandy elbowed him. "Hey."

"Ow," he said, but kissed her temple.

"It's fine," Malcom said with a laugh, although it was sort of a bitter one. "I've been told that a lot—by ladies mostly—that I'm a workaholic." He shrugged and finished the last of his water. "I honestly don't mind living on site, and I suppose that makes me one. And to answer the dating question, it's just easier not to date. You know—avoid the awkward end-of-the-evening stuff."

Ian smirked. Brandy elbowed him again. "Well, you'd get along perfectly with Lori, then," he said. "She doesn't date either."

"Ian, I'm going to staple your mouth shut." Brandy looked at Lori. "I'm sorry, hon. I'm taking him upstairs to find a place to lock him up." And with that she tugged him with her.

"Sorry, Lori," Ian said, sounding contrite. "I'm totally kidding." He looked at Malcom. "You should come up for our barbecue tomorrow afternoon, Malcom. The more the merrier." He gave a significant look in Lori's direction as his voice trailed off.

"We'll see," Malcom said, surprised he'd been invited in the first place.

Ian and Brandy disappeared out of the kitchen, and Malcom straightened from the counter and looked over at Lori. She didn't look embarrassed exactly, but there seemed to be more color in her cheeks.

"How is it that some men can revert to a ten-year-old boy at a moment's notice?" she said in a matter-of-fact voice. "No offense to your gender."

Malcom raised both his hands. "None taken. I guess I walked right into that one. Sorry you got dragged into the mud too."

Lori wrapped her fingers around the end of her ponytail. "I might have cared once, or been offended, but he's right. So what's the point of contradicting him?"

This was interesting. "You really don't date?"

She lifted a shoulder. "I don't currently date. It's not like I'm a nun, or anything. I just kept hitting dead ends, so about a year ago, I stopped swiping on those apps. I forbade my friends to set me up. I stopped going to those singles' meetups."

"Sounds painful."

Lori winced. "You have no idea."

They were basically alone downstairs, and all seemed quiet. "I'm up for a good story." Now that he had her talking, he wanted to hear more from her—about anything.

Lori hesitated. "It's late, and I'm sure you want to head home. Or to your trailer, whatever you call it."

"Trailer is fine." He couldn't help but smile. "And I'm a night owl. Also, I love stories."

Lori shifted in her seat and leaned forward on her elbows. Her lips curved into a sweet smile. "I'll tell you one story, then."

"Perfect." He moved around the counter and sat one stool away from her. Not too close, but not far either.

"I only remember this because it was right after I opened my shop," she said. "About six months ago—"

"It's your shop, then? You own it?"

"Yeah, it's my shop." She paused, but when he didn't say anything more, she continued. "We'd had an unexpectedly busy day, so I only had a few minutes to get ready. I decided to stay in my regular clothes—pink pants, white top, and Easter egg earrings. You know, because of the holiday."

He smiled.

"But I had to touch up my makeup, you know, so I wouldn't scare any potential dates off."

"Dates?"

"The event was one of those speed-dating things."

He nodded, even though he'd never been to one, and didn't think he could be paid to attend. Also, he was pretty sure Lori looked fine with no makeup—was she even wearing any now? Because she looked perfectly fine.

"I arrived to find that they had a bunch of tables set up." Lori gave a half smile. "The women stayed put, and the men moved from table to table. Everyone had five minutes to chat, then a timer would go off, and the men would shuffle to the next woman at the next table." She drew in a breath. "Each one felt like a painful job interview—but with rapid-fire personal questions."

Malcom was totally invested. "Questions like what's your favorite color?"

Lori laughed softly. "Those would have been welcome. No, the questions were about my age, how many kids did I want, where did I want to live when I married, what my parents were like, what income level did I have . . ."

"Wow, to the point, I guess," he mused. "I mean those are things that will eventually come out, but maybe not in a fire hose of questions."

"Exactly." Lori sighed. "Despite all of that, I gave my number to three of the men. They all called, but nothing went beyond a first date. In fact, nothing has gone beyond a first date for years." She shrugged and traced a finger along the marble lines on the island. "When I even think about going on a date now, I just shut down. I have no interest, and I'd rather do anything else—even go to the dentist."

Malcom laughed. "That's kind of depressing, but I totally get it."

Lori tilted her head, her mouth turning up. "So you're not going to shame me?"

"Not at all." He glanced toward the stairs that Brandy and Ian had taken. "I can't say the same for any of your friends, but relationships aren't for everyone. I'm perfectly happy and functional and marginally successful in life."

She was fully smiling now. "You are. And I don't think either of us should change for other people. We can just be ourselves. Single and happy."

"Right. Single and happy." Malcom folded his arms. "So what about your family? Do you have any siblings?"

"No siblings." She gave him a quick rundown of her parents selling their hardware store, moving to Florida, and leaving her to fix up their house to sell.

Malcom whistled. "Wow, that's a lot. You're fixing the place up by yourself?"

At her nod, he asked, "When do you sleep?"

She smirked. "Between midnight and six?"

"So we're probably past your bedtime now?"

Lori laughed. "Yeah." Then she stifled a yawn.

He stood from the island and retrieved his tool bag. "Thanks for telling me your story. I should get going, Sleeping Beauty."

"Anytime," Lori said, her cheeks taking on a faint pink. "But maybe not at one in the morning."

"Is it that late already?" Malcom pulled out his phone. He had several texts from Penny and a couple from Jay. Nothing from his date.

Lori had moved to the front door and opened it.

He headed toward her. "It was great talking to you. Thanks for not making me feel like the odd man out."

"I'm sure you'll date when you're ready or you find that perfect woman." Lori leaned against the door, her eyes bright. "Don't let anyone tell you otherwise."

"It's a deal," he said. "And the same goes for you. Although, I must say, those one-date men were missing out."

"Oh really? Do you think they should have asked me out on a second date?" Lori teased.

"Definitely. Their loss."

Her cheeks had flushed again, and Malcom was strangely happy knowing that maybe she took his compliment to heart. Because it was only the truth.

"Well, thanks, and hope you drive safe."

"I'll be fine." He stepped out onto the porch in the crisp night air. The stars above seemed to spread for miles.

"And what should I tell Ian about tomorrow's barbecue?" Lori asked.

He was surprised she brought it up, but also pleased. It would have been awkward showing up. Ian hadn't even told him a time. But now that Lori was asking . . . it felt more like an invitation he couldn't turn down. "What time is the barbeque?"

"Around six." She tilted her head. "Do you have any free time? I mean, you are the boss."

"I am the boss . . . which means I can make my own schedule."

Her smile appeared. He really liked that feature of hers.

"You should come," she said in a breezy tone. "All the guys

are great, even when they act like ten-year-olds. And if you're going to be around Everly Falls for a few months, you might want more options than hanging out in your trailer."

"And you think a barbecue is a good place to start?" Malcom knew he was borderline flirting now, but Lori didn't seem to mind.

"I think it's an excellent place to start." She tucked a bit of flyaway hair that had escaped her ponytail behind her ear. "But I must warn you. Once the others find out you're single, they'll probably try to set you up with someone."

"Like you?" Malcom said, toeing the line.

Lori laughed. "No, we can nip that in the bud right from the start. We still have plenty of high school friends who fit the single status."

"Ah. Well, then, I think I'm going to stick to your strategy." Malcom smiled. "No blind dates for me. If I meet someone, it has to be organically."

"Good plan," Lori said, moving a step away from him. "Have a good night and see you at the barbecue—if you come."

Malcom nodded, about to turn away. Then he paused. "I wanted to ask you about the cat earrings. Do you have a bunch of cats or something who are like your children?"

Lori's brows shot up. "Are you calling me a cat lady?"

"If the shoe fits . . ."

Thankfully, she smiled, and he was glad he hadn't put his foot in his mouth—too much.

"I do love cats," she said, idly twisting one of the cat earrings. "I don't currently have one, if you must know, but it's all part of the ruse. Keeps away the guys looking for a hookup. They see my holiday earrings and assume I'm a bit odd—which you just verified—and they walk the other way as fast as possible."

"You know that a lot of men love cats too."

Lori puffed out a breath. "In those cases, I tell them I'm already in a relationship. They just don't have to know that it's with myself."

"Ouch." Malcom brought a hand to his chest. "I'm glad you don't tell those poor men that you'd rather be alone than with them."

"Alone is a relative term," she said. "Am I really alone? Not exactly. I mean, I'm alone in my bed at night, but that's for sleeping anyway. Otherwise, I'm always with someone. I wouldn't consider myself lonely, if you know what I mean."

"I do." Malcom had never had such a varied and interesting conversation in all his life. He was really glad Brandy and Ian had ditched them. He really should go though, or he'd find himself talking to her for another hour. "See you tomorrow, Lori. Maybe."

She laughed, and as he headed down the stairs, he heard the door click softly behind him.

# Five

THE DAY HAD BEEN WONDERFUL—fun and restful—and the only annoying thing was that Brandy had told all their friends Malcom Graves was making eyes at Lori the night before. Which wasn't true at all. Lori had thought he was definitely solicitous and attentive—but she chalked that up to his personality more than anything. He ran a construction company, and he had to deal with employees and people all day long. So of course he knew how to listen and make the other person feel genuinely heard.

"I think I'm going to read for a little bit," Lori told her friends. "Unless you still need my help."

"We're totally good," Julie said.

They'd just finished prepping a couple of salads to go along with dinner, and Dave and Ian would be starting on the meat in about an hour.

"What are you reading?" Stephenie asked, leaning on the counter across from her. "Anything good?"

"I brought a few selections," Lori said. "But I think I'm going to start the mystery I brought, *The Thursday Murder Club*. Heard only good things."

"Oh, I've read that series," Steph said. "Excellent fun."

Julie's frown appeared. "How is a murder mystery fun?"

"It's a cozy mystery series—kind of amateur sleuth stuff," Stephenie said. "Quirky characters who are endearing."

"What's endearing?" Cal asked, coming into the kitchen. He settled an arm across Stephenie's shoulders.

"We're just talking about books," she said, leaning against him.

Cal pressed a kiss on her cheek.

Time for Lori to go. "Let me know if you need anything." She headed out of the kitchen and up the stairs. Her bedroom overlooked the back of the house, and if she stood at the right angle, she could see the deck. She settled onto the bed and grabbed the mystery novel. Before she dove in, she texted Marci for an update. A reply came immediately.

*Steady traffic, but not so busy that I can't handle it. Mostly selling Halloween decor.*

*Great,* Lori texted back. She was happy people were buying the Halloween stuff—it meant she'd made the right ordering decisions. She set her phone aside and opened the novel.

Somehow time flew by, and she was just figuring out who all the characters were when she heard male voices outside the cabin. Maybe the men were starting up the barbecue? She had to check . . . in case . . . Climbing off the bed, she crossed to the window and looked down at the deck.

Dave, Ian, and Cal were all on the deck. Yep, starting up the barbecue. As she watched, Austin came outside, and with him, another man wearing a ball cap.

Lori's heart stuttered. It was Malcom. She knew it, even with the ball cap on.

He'd come after all.

She moved back a step in case someone looked up and spotted her. But she couldn't stop spying on them—or him, more specifically. He wore a T-shirt and shorts, and he seemed to be intermixing with the other guys quite easily. She couldn't hear what they were saying, but there was definitely laughter.

Lori's pulse continued to race, which it had no business doing. She and Malcom had an interesting conversation last night, that was all. She moved to the en suite bathroom and checked her appearance. She undid her ponytail and smoothed her hair, then put it up again. Black-and-silver spider earrings dangled from her earlobes. They were one of her favorite pairs. She'd actually worn them on one of her dates last year. He had said he hated spiders.

By the time she came out of the bathroom and looked out the window again, the women had joined the men. Well, that meant it was time for her to go downstairs. She didn't want anyone coming to look for her. Drawing a deep breath and shaking away any nervous thoughts—which were ridiculous—she headed downstairs, then slipped out onto the deck.

She crossed to the rail and perched next to it, acting interested in the conversation going on around her. Brandy was in the midst of the men, and the other women were talking about Julie's kids.

"Oh, here's a funny one of Maren when she was trying to feed her baby brother goldfish crackers." Julie held out her phone and the women passed it from one to the other.

"So you took the picture, then took way the goldfish?" Everly teased.

"Well, yeah." Julie laughed and retrieved her phone. "Bad mom?"

"I'm not going to judge anyone's parenting," Everly said. "I mean, I'm still trying to figure out the ropes of being a stepmom."

The conversation morphed into talking about seven-year-old Jessica, who was Austin's daughter. He was widowed, so now Everly was mom and stepmom.

"Oh, there you are," Brandy said, turning away from the guys and spotting Lori.

Lori smiled over at her friend. She really didn't want to be singled out, and she could only pray that Brandy wouldn't put her on the spot about something. But Brandy just sat in a nearby chair and added to the conversation about how adorable and smart Jessica was. "I swear she's going to be a lawyer or politician someday," she said with a laugh. "That girl's got some negotiating skills."

Lori laughed too—she'd definitely been witness to that. Just then, Malcom separated from the group of men. Maybe she'd been watching him, but it hadn't been intentional.

"Hey," he said. "How are you?"

Well, that quieted all of the women, so everyone heard her answer. "Great. Glad you decided to come."

Lori hoped her voice sounded normal . . . Did it sound normal? She didn't feel normal. Her pulse was jumping around again. Malcom's hazel eyes were more green than brown in the light of the setting sun. His shirt looked like it had been painted on, although it wasn't exactly tight. It just defined every bit of his shoulders and upper arms and torso. Lori wasn't one to ogle a man's body, but Malcom was hard to look away from. Which was, again, ridiculous. Lori had gone on plenty of dates with athletic men. She'd even dated a body builder—well, one time—whose neck was larger than her thigh.

"I got my brother to fill in on the maintenance calls today for this community," Malcom said. "After all, it was his sister-in-law who put together the contract without giving me a heads-up."

So . . . he was picking up from last night's conversation, and her friends were all here for it, soaking in every word.

"That's only fair, right?" Lori said, feeling self-conscious and probably blushing as well. "Do you guys split the company fifty-fifty?"

"On paper, yes." Malcom finished crossing the distance and leaned on the railing a couple feet from her. There were plenty of chairs around, but it seemed he wasn't going to take one.

"What does that mean?" She might as well continue talking to him. First, she was interested in his answers, and second, her friends were still basically staring at him.

"Bronson's wife helps out on a part-time basis, but her opinion carries plenty of weight," he said, folding his arms, which of course made them more defined.

Heavens.

"We put her on payroll a few months ago, even though she kept trying to tell us not to," Malcom said. "She's kind of stubborn."

Lori smiled. "Sounds like it. But you're a standup person to do that."

"We'll see after today," he said. "She might resent their weekend plans being interrupted."

"Oh wow, yeah," Lori said. "Did they have big plans?"

"She said no, but she always has something planned." His gaze stayed on her—as it had been from the moment he started talking to her. Did he not know they had an audience?

"Well, hopefully this barbecue will be delicious enough to justify a family dispute."

Malcom laughed.

Heavens again. Had she not noticed his dimples before? Okay, so she'd noticed, but she was trying not to add to his list of qualities. Physical stuff was just icing on the cake anyway. It didn't give longevity to relationships.

"I'll let you know," he said, his laugh still dancing in his eyes.

"Perfect," she said with a smile. And somehow she knew he wasn't teasing. He *would* let her know. Would he get her number and text her? Would he come over to the shop? Would she randomly see him outside? They were kind of neighbors . . .

"I like the spiders," he said.

It took her a minute before she realized what he meant. "Oh, thanks." She touched one of her earrings, feeling the small dangling legs.

"She wears all kinds of bugs on her ears," Julie said. "My three-year-old is fascinated by them."

"Not *all kinds* of bugs," Lori said. "These spider ones, sure. I have ants too. Otherwise I have things like dragonflies and butterflies."

"Ants? When do you wear those?" Malcom asked. "Oh wait, let me guess." He pretended to think. "Hiking? To a picnic?"

Lori grinned. "Pretty much. You'd make a good detective."

Brandy joined them at the rail, while the other women fell into their own conversation. "You should see her on Halloween night," she said with a glint in her eye. "She dresses up like a witch, and no one recognizes her."

Malcom's brows raised. "What kind of witch?"

Lori was speechless for a moment. No one had ever asked her that. "I'm a nice witch, of course," she said. "More of a fortune teller, really."

"I'll bet the kids love that."

"She has lines out the door," Brandy said.

His dimples were back. "Looking forward to seeing it."

Lori's pulse jumped another notch. Of course he'd still be around at the end of October. How long would the building project take? Several months at least.

"The first batch of hamburgers is ready," Dave announced. "The steaks and chicken will take a little longer."

"What are you having?" Malcom asked.

"Oh, um, I'll wait for the chicken." She made eye contact with Brandy, who had a big smile on her face. "But you help yourself if you want a hamburger," she told him.

He moved off to get his burger, and Brandy didn't wait even a half a minute before saying in a whisper, "He's *interested* in you."

"No, he's not," Lori said immediately, keeping her voice quiet too.

The women had fallen silent again. "What's this?" Everly asked.

"Nothing," Lori replied at the same time that Brandy said, "Malcom hasn't paid attention to anyone except for Lori since the moment she came outside."

"Ooo." Stephenie quirked a smile. "I can see it. I can definitely see it. You two would make a good match."

"None of us even know him," Lori protested. "Not really. Just because he's single, and I'm single, doesn't mean we need to automatically start dating."

"You forgot to mention that he's hot," Brandy said with a wink.

Lori hoped her face wasn't turning red. "Which would prove my point even more. I'm not interested in players." She knew he wasn't a player—well, she didn't think he was. He didn't give off that vibe, and from their conversation last night, she'd ruled that out. "Besides, who else is he going to talk to when everyone else has a plus one except for me?"

Her friends were all staring at her, in various stages of speculation and amusement.

"We're just teasing," Brandy said, although she looked like she was about to laugh.

"Oh, he just glanced over here," Julie said, her voice a low rumble. "Don't look now, but he's definitely checking out Lori."

"I'll bet he asks for your number before the barbecue is over," Stephenie added.

All of the women grinned, anticipation in their eyes.

Lori was officially annoyed. They weren't teenagers anymore, and they all knew about her bad dating experiences and her current hiatus. Actually, she was more than annoyed. She felt emotion burning in her chest, which was ridiculous. But she wasn't going to survive this barbecue if all of her friends were watching and speculating. Someone would say something embarrassing, like Ian had last night, and she just wasn't up for it.

"Hey, I need to grab something inside," she said, and walked away before anyone could question her.

She had nothing to grab inside, unless it was her sanity, because her emotions were simmering. Why was she so upset? These were her best friends. They razzed each other all the time. What made this any different? She was being too sensitive, and she knew it, but that didn't stop her eyes from burning as she walked through the cabin. She didn't stop until she reached the front porch. Settling onto the hanging porch swing, she forced herself to take some calming breaths.

If she were completely honest with herself, the only reason she was reacting like this was because she had enjoyed her time with Malcom last night. And she had been flattered when he'd come over and chatted with her just now. He was a cool guy. She liked talking to him. He was interesting, attentive, and yes, he was good-looking. But there was a lot more to him than that. And it wasn't like Lori was hoping to date him, though she would like to get to know him better.

But not on stage with everyone watching and putting in their two cents.

She texted Marci for any store updates. Marci wrote back that she was just getting ready to close, and everything had gone well that day. Plenty of sales. Lori typed back that she'd check inventory when she returned the next day to see about reordering the things that had been popular.

She pocketed her phone, feeling a little disappointed that she wasn't needed. There wasn't any emergency reason for her to return—like a broken pipe. Not that she'd be any good with fixing anything like that—Malcom probably would. But that was neither here nor there.

She closed her eyes and used her toes to push back on the swing, gently rocking it back and forth. It was peaceful out front, and she could hear the rise and fall of murmured conversation from around the house, but it wasn't disruptive.

When the front door opened, Lori opened her eyes, realizing she'd dozed off.

Malcom walked out onto the porch with a plate of food in his hands. "There you are. Your friends thought maybe you'd be in your bedroom, but I thought I'd check here first."

# Six

MALCOM HAD REALIZED A SECOND too late that Lori was sleeping. Her eyes flew open when he opened the door, so he continued onto the porch, a plate of dinner in his hands. He'd seen her leave the back deck maybe thirty minutes ago. The group of friends didn't seem to be bothered with her not returning after a few minutes. Malcom wasn't bothered either. Just curious. Was she preparing more food in the kitchen? Gathering more drinks?

He wasn't exactly watching the time, but when the chicken came off the grill, and she still didn't return, he finally asked one of the women—Everly—if Lori was coming back.

"Oh, you should go look for her," Everly said, a wide smile on her face. "See if she needs help with anything. Maybe she went to her bedroom?"

All the women smiled at him. What was going on?

Malcom waited a few more minutes, and when Lori still didn't show, he loaded up a plate of food and carried it into the house. He didn't bother to look to see if anyone was watching him, or wondering what he was doing.

Inside, the cabin was quiet. It felt intrusive to start knocking on bedroom doors. Then he noticed a porch swing through the front windows. Maybe it was a hunch that led him out the front door. But there she was. Curled against the cushioned swing, her legs tucked up, her eyes closed.

Before he could backtrack, she opened her eyes.

He tried to explain himself, and she blinked a few times, as if trying to remember why she was sleeping on the porch.

"Sorry," he continued. "I didn't mean to wake you. I can save this for later."

She slid her legs down so she was in a regular sitting position. Her cheeks were slightly flushed, and her eyes looked sleepy—sexy, really, but he wouldn't let his thoughts go there.

"I didn't mean to fall asleep," she said, stifling a yawn. "It's just so peaceful out here, and I didn't get to bed until late last night."

He nodded because he knew why.

Her smile appeared. "You brought me food? Or is that for you?"

Malcom chuckled. "It's for you. The chicken was done a while ago, so it might not be warm anymore." He moved closer to her. "Do you want it out here? Or to go join the others?"

Lori eyed the plate. He'd even brought utensils and a water bottle.

"Right here would be great. Join me? I think there's enough for two."

"Oh, I ate." Malcom handed her the plate. "Want company? Or are you by yourself for a reason?"

"Have a seat," Lori said, shifting over a little.

The swing swayed, and Malcom steadied it, then sat down. There was plenty of room between them, but that didn't stop him from being aware of how close they were in fact sitting. She smelled nice. Like sweet apples. Was it her shampoo?

"If it's too cold, I can take it to the microwave," he said.

"Oh, it's fine," she said, taking a bite. "Thank you so much."

His phone buzzed, but he ignored it. He should have turned the thing off. "I didn't know what you like, so I dished up a little of everything."

Lori laughed. "I noticed. I mean, I like it all, but there's a lot. Even if I were starving, this is more of a man's portion. Not to be sexist or anything."

"Hmm," he said. "Some women eat bigger meals—especially those who are intermittently fasting like my sister-in-law. She eats more than my brother, but he also snacks."

"That's me," Lori said. "I'm definitely a snacker. I think all readers are. A good book is even better with snacks."

"Oh really?" He found himself smiling. "Is that a rule or something? Maybe I'd enjoy reading more if I'd known about the snacks."

"You for sure would." Lori took a bite of her salad. "What was the last book you read?"

That made him pause. "Uh . . . can I get back to you on that? Unless articles on a news app count?"

"That definitely doesn't count," she said with a smirk. "Do you like a certain genre? Business books? Novels? Thrillers?"

"Not business books, although I should probably read some," he said. "I went through a Tom Clancy stage in my early twenties."

She nodded, looking pleased. "So there's hope. I mean, if you've liked a certain author or genre in the past, then that's at least a starting place."

Malcom chuckled. "I'm flattered that you think I can be redeemed."

Lori's gaze connected with his, and he saw the interest there—it was unmistakable. And probably relatable too, because he was definitely interested in her. As a friend, of course. They'd both agreed they weren't looking to date anyone, so that pressure was off. They could just hang out and talk about books he'd never read.

"If you want any recommendations, I have plenty," Lori continued, then took another bite of the chicken. Her earrings swayed with the movement. "But I don't want to come at you like a fire hose."

Malcom had to laugh at this. "I really appreciate your consideration."

"No problem." She held up her plate. "Want anything? I'm full."

He eyed the food. There was still at least half of it left. He could eat more. He hadn't eaten all day except for a protein bar that morning. "I'll eat some."

She handed over the plate, then held up the fork. "Should I grab you a new one?"

"Are you sick or anything?" he asked, mostly teasing.

"Nope. But I could be carrying something. You never know."

"I can risk a few cooties."

Lori laughed, which made him smile. He liked her laughter.

His phone buzzed again, but he still ignored it. He wasn't too worried since the job site was closed today, so it wasn't any sort of emergency. Maybe it was his brother? Or more likely Penny asking if he had plans tonight. Or maybe it was Jay wanting to talk about the night before, when Malcom had bailed early on their double date.

Lori drew her feet up under her again as he finished off her plate—he was hungrier than he thought. She handed over her half-filled water bottle and he finished that off too.

"Thanks again," she said. "It's nice to be waited on."

He felt his smile appear. "You're welcome." Just then, his phone rang. A text he could ignore, but phone calls usually meant something was more urgent.

"You can get it," Lori said.

He pulled the phone out of his pocket. Bronson's name glowed on the screen. "It's my brother," he said, right before answering.

"Dude, where've you been?" Bronson said. "I've been trying to reach you. I'm heading out for the rest of the weekend, and I need you to fix a broken gate latch at one of those cabins. Then stay on-call for Sunday. Sorry I have to bail. But Monday, we'll have Rick be the man."

"I thought you agreed with Penny to be on-call the entire weekend," Malcom said. "This was a deal between you and her. Not me."

"You and I are partners, though, not Penny," Bronson said. "I'm not going to bail on my wife."

"Kari told me you didn't have any plans."

Bronson chuckled. "You know women. They get to change their minds. Anyway, I'll text you the work order. Sorry to bail, but I'll owe you one, and that's never a bad thing."

"You owe me a lot more than one—" he started to say, but Bronson had already hung up.

Malcom exhaled in frustration. He stared at his phone for a couple of seconds, trying to wrap his head around the fact that his brother and sister-in-law had put him in this position. He already worked weekdays on the job site from sunup to sundown. He didn't mind weekend work, when it was for his project. This new maintenance contract had never been his idea, but now apparently he was stuck with it.

"You have to go be Mr. Fix-It again?" Lori asked.

He turned his head. "Yeah, sorry. There's been some miscommunication going on between my brother and me lately. Bronson's wife Kari and her sister Penny in the mix makes things even more complicated." He rose to his feet, plate in hand. "I guess my break is over."

"I'm sorry." Lori moved to her feet as well and faced him.

"Here, I can throw this away. Can you come back after? I'm sure all the guys want you to stick around. How long does fixing a gate latch take?"

"I can't say until I look at it," Malcom said. "I have tools in my truck, but if it needs to be replaced, I'll have to head into town to the hardware store. If it's even still open."

"It closes at six on Saturday night, like every night," she said. "But I know Gil, the owner, and he could let us in."

Malcom stared at Lori. "Really? I mean, that would be great." He paused. "Wait. You don't need to come."

She gave him a small smile. "I kind of want to come. I mean, not on your errands, but maybe you can drop me off at my place when you get back to town? I'm sort of over being the only solo person at this retreat."

Surprise rippled through him. "I thought they were all your best friends."

"Oh, they are. And they've all matched up with great guys." She lifted a shoulder. "I don't know. My head's not in it, and I don't want to bring anyone down."

Malcom didn't know what to say here, how to respond, but if she wanted a ride back to town, he didn't mind giving her one. "You're okay with checking out that gate first?"

Lori nodded. "I'm not in a hurry. I just . . . wouldn't mind leaving here earlier than tomorrow."

"Okay. No problem."

"I'll be really fast in packing up," Lori said, squeezing his hand, then letting go. "Just give me a couple of minutes."

Before he could say anything more, she went inside to the kitchen and dumped the plate and empty water bottle into the trash. Then she hurried up the stairs, leaving him standing in the entryway, feeling the lingering warmth from her hand on his.

He headed to the kitchen and perched on a stool. While

he waited for Lori to pack, Brandy and Ian came inside, carrying a couple of empty platters.

"Did you find her?" Brandy asked.

"Yeah," Malcom said. "But I've got to take off. I guess I'm still the on-call maintenance guy, and I've got a gate to fix."

Ian frowned. "Oh, sorry about that. Do you want me to come help you?"

"It's fine," he said.

"I'm helping him." Lori appeared in the kitchen, carrying a duffle bag. "I'm also going back tonight. He's dropping me off. Sorry I can't stay longer."

Brandy's gaze widened. "You're *leaving*? We've got a bunch of stuff planned for tonight and tomorrow."

"I know, and I'm sorry to dash off," Lori told her, not looking sorry at all. "Marci said the store was super busy today, so I've got to go through inventory and put in new orders ASAP."

Brandy's frown appeared, and Malcom knew she wasn't buying that story. But she stepped forward to hug her friend anyway. "Well, we'll miss you," she said, her gaze shifting to Malcom over Lori's shoulder. "Drive safe, you two."

"Tell everyone bye for me." Lori stepped away from Brandy, then started walking toward the door.

Malcom watched her swift walk. She meant business. "Okay. Well. See you all later. Thanks for everything."

"See you at the gym Monday?" Ian said.

"I'll be there."

Malcom headed out of the kitchen and found Lori waiting for him on the front porch. "You don't want to say goodbye to the rest of your friends?"

She waved a hand. "I'll see them soon enough. Besides, I don't need everyone fussing over me."

"Makes sense." He reached for the duffle. "I can carry that."

He noticed her hesitation, but then she relinquished it. The weight surprised him. "Wow, it's heavy."

She shrugged. "Books."

"Should have guessed."

He liked the way the edges of her eyes lifted when she smiled. Once they reached his truck, he opened the passenger door, and she climbed in. Then he set the duffle on the back seat. As he walked around the truck, he wondered why she was so keen on leaving the weekend retreat. With him, no less. Surely one of her friends would have driven her back if necessary. Well, he wasn't going to pester her about it.

"Thanks for this," Lori said, when he settled into the driver's seat. "You're saving me."

"From what?" he asked, genuinely curious. He pulled up the text from Bronson with the work order, and plugged in the address of the cabin.

She heaved out a sigh. "From another twenty-four hours of being the odd man—or woman—out. I was trying to not let it bother me, and for the most part it didn't, but when you showed up—"

"Wait, this has something to do with me?"

"Not *you* specifically," Lori said with an apologetic smile. "But it was the fact that you're single too. And I'm the last holdout, apparently, so my friends decided that we should immediately fall in love and live happily ever after."

"Wow, no pressure there." Malcom pulled out of the circular driveway. He glanced over at her. She was gazing out the window, biting her lower lip, her shoulders tense. "So you didn't want to deal with the aftermath when I left the barbecue without proposing?"

She looked over at him and smirked. "Something like that. I guess I didn't want the weekend to be all about 'what should we do about Lori' and 'how can we get Lori and

Malcom to go out on a date?'" She waved a hand. "Who knows what they'll think of my driving off with you though."

"You'll just have to set them straight," Malcom said as he slowed the truck, then turned onto the main canyon road. "Tell them you helped me fix a gate, then I took you straight home. No declarations of love and no proposals."

He knew he was grinning, and it made his heart light when she grinned back.

# Seven

LORI HAD JUST FINISHED PAINTING one wall in her childhood bedroom in her parents' old house when her cell rang. She dabbed her hands on a drop cloth and picked up Marci's call.

"Sorry to interrupt," Marci said, "but I'm really not feeling well. I thought I could stick it out, but I feel like I'm going to puke any second."

Lori winced. "Sorry you're sick. I'll head over right now. If you need to just leave, lock the door. It won't be a big deal if the place is locked up for a short time."

"Thank you," Marci said in a strained voice. "Sorry again."

Then she was gone, and Lori turned to survey her latest round of painting. She'd decided to paint all of the walls in the house a mellow taupe color. Everly and Austin had done a walk-through and suggested a few easy updates in order to make the house more appealing to buyers. "Easy" was a relative word. Well, okay, painting was easy in general, but very time consuming if one wanted to do it right.

Lori closed up the paint can, cleaned the roller, then headed out of the house.

By the time she got to the store, Marci was gone—which Lori was grateful for. She sent a quick text. *I'm at the store now. Hope you feel better soon.*

She unlocked the door, and once inside, straightened a few things. It was the usual two p.m. lull in the store when no none came in. The morning shoppers were long gone, and the lunch rush over with. In about an hour, with school getting out, more shoppers would come. Teenagers included. Most would browse. If they bought anything, it would be something like a spider ring, or a bag of candy.

With Marci not around, things were quiet save for the music track of Halloween songs and the occasional rumble of construction machinery across the street.

Speaking of construction . . . it had been two weeks since Lori had seen Malcom. Not that she was exactly keeping track. Oh, she'd caught a glimpse of him a time or two—when she was peering out her shop window, or even her apartment window on the second floor. But those had been happenstance sightings. He seemed really busy. Always moving about the job site, talking to people, going in and out of the trailer. She still marveled that he slept there.

A couple times when she'd awakened in the middle of the night to get a drink, she'd glanced out the window to see that there was a light on inside the trailer. Did he never sleep? Or did he sleep with the light on? That thought made her giggle.

Her friends had finally stopped pestering her about the drive home from the cabin. Her story remained the same each time they'd asked, so they'd eventually moved on to other topics.

Lori moved about the store, aimlessly straightening things while she let her mind wander. On the drive home from the cabin, Malcom took only about fifteen minutes to repair the gate. He didn't have to buy a new latch after all. So she was back at her store in a short time. They hadn't exchanged numbers or anything, and why should they?

Lori paused by the front window. There was some extra

activity going on across the way. People in regular clothes approaching the trailer.

Malcom stepped out the door and lifted a hand in greeting, then descended the few steps. There were two women with a man, and they all stood around talking for a few moments.

Lori stepped back from the window; she really shouldn't be watching, or spying. But she continued anyway.

One of the women moved closer to Malcom and put her hand on his arm. He smiled at her, but even from this distance, Lori could tell it was strained. The woman was dressed to the nines in a lavender suit, blonde hair waving down her back, three-inch-minimum high heels that were red.

The other man and the other woman walked toward the building site, hand in hand. So they were together. But blondie lingered with Malcom, and they seemed to be in a vigorous discussion. Lori's curiosity only grew.

When the man turned back to motion toward Malcom, she saw the resemblance. Several things clicked into place. The man was his brother, Bronson, and that must be the brother's wife, Kari.

Lori's mind spun, trying to keep the relationships in order. The blonde woman giving her full attention to Malcom had to be Penny.

And if Lori wasn't mistaken, Penny was very, very interested in Malcom.

At that moment, he put some distance between him and Penny as he followed after his brother. She did her best to keep up in those heels of hers.

Lori turned away. None of this was her business. She did feel a little sorry for Malcom, but he could handle his own family. He'd been doing it a while. She moved to the counter, where she arranged Halloween lollipops on a graveyard display. The lollipops were surprisingly popular. Maybe not too surprising. Lori loved them as well. She unwrapped one and popped it into her mouth. One of the benefits of being the store owner, she supposed.

She'd bought this store about six months ago, and every day she was grateful. That should say something, right? She could make good choices, after all, that didn't fall under the circle of her parents. Her dad had owned the hardware store most of her life, and when he sold it, Lori had felt out of sorts. She'd been working there since she was a kid—doing odd jobs at first, then given a more official position after a couple years at a community college.

She'd always thought she might take over the store one day.

Instead, her dad sold it, and said if he didn't, he'd never be able to truly retire. He'd invested a portion of the sale into her own shop. Then her parents were off to Florida. They hadn't invited her to move with them. Okay, so she should admit it— living with her parents in Everly Falls had been convenient, but not ideal. And maybe it had taken them moving out of state, and wanting to sell their house, to finally get a place of her own.

If that had been their plan, it had worked.

It also, she realized now, might have caused some of her dating hangups. Living with her parents didn't exactly equate to any romantic nights. But none of that had happened anyway, even once she was on her own. So she couldn't blame her living situation any longer.

Speaking of parents . . . her phone rang, and her mom's number lit up the screen. Lori knew better than to ignore the call if she could help it. Her mom only called when there was an emergency—most of which could be taken with a grain of salt. A few days ago, she had called because she'd lost her credit card. What was Lori supposed to do about it?

Regardless, her mom had been in a panic, so Lori looked up the credit card company's number for her and sent it over. She'd been tempted to tell her it was a good thing for Dad to help out with, but he was terrible at financial stuff and would think there was some sort of conspiracy theory working against them if the credit company asked Mom to verify some personal data.

Okay, maybe Lori was really grateful that she no longer lived with her parents.

"Hi, Mom," she answered in a cheerful tone, even though her stomach had tightened with trepidation.

"Oh, thank goodness you answered," her mom said. "I got the strangest text about the post office delivering something, but they didn't have my address. Dad told me to call and see if you've sent us anything?"

Lori swallowed back a sigh. "Mom, if it were me, I'd have your address. The text is a scam. Remember the last one you got from UPS?"

"Yeah, but this was from USPS—they're different, honey."

"It's still a scam."

"Are you sure?" her mom pressed.

"I'm sure," Lori insisted. "Just delete it. Don't open the link or give out any information to a random number, no matter what they claim."

"I know, you're right." Her mom paused. "How is everything going?"

"Just busy at the store—Halloween is coming up."

"Oh, of course. Any updates on your dating life?"

Lori closed her eyes for a second. "No updates." Her mom didn't need to ask the same question every phone call. "If there's a change, I'll let you know. I should run—the school crowd will be here soon."

She hung up, hoping that her mom would stop taking

scam texts seriously. But Lori was glad she had called anyway. She picked up the lollipop again.

The bell over the door jangled, and Lori looked over to see Malcom. His tall frame filled the doorway, and he looked a bit hesitant. When their gazes met, he stepped across the threshold. "Hey."

She popped the lollipop out of her mouth. "Hey."

"You open?" He looked around at the empty store.

"Yeah, of course." She glanced at the witch-hat clock on the wall. "Just kind of the dead hour."

"Sorry I've been kind of a stranger," he said, moving toward the counter where she stood. His navy ball cap hooded his hazel eyes. Everything else was his usual attire—T-shirt, well-worn jeans, and boots. "I mean, you've been a stranger too."

Why was her pulse jumping about? And they were strangers—mostly. They'd had a few conversations, but she didn't expect them to continue. She didn't think they'd start hanging out or anything. "I've been busy, and I'm guessing you've been swamped."

"Yeah." He looked about the store again, and she almost laughed.

"I mean, I'm not busy at this exact moment," Lori clarified. "But there's always something to organize or restock. Plus, in about twenty minutes, this place will be crawling with teenagers."

Malcom leaned a hand on the counter between them. "Oh, I believe you. I came at this time on purpose."

She raised her brows at this. "Because you knew it was the dead hour?"

"I can be observant sometimes." His voice was a low rumble, and her pulse leapt again. His gaze shifted from her face to her clothing. "I like your shirt."

Lori looked down, even though she knew which shirt she wore: *I'm Only a Witch in the Mornings.*

"And your earrings," he added.

She smiled and touched the miniature black-and-purple witch hats. "They match the shirt."

His gaze roamed her face, and something in his eyes told her he approved. His scrutiny made her pulse jump. Soon, she'd be blushing.

"Have you been painting?" he asked.

*How can he tell?* Then Lori saw the paint streaks on her left wrist. "Oh." She rubbed at it, making the paint flecks fall off. "Yeah. I was painting my old bedroom at my parents' house. Decided to go with one color for the whole house—you know, instead of the green in my parents' bedroom, the pink in my room, and the yellow in the kitchen."

Malcom smiled, which showed off his dimples. "Color brings personality to the house."

"Yeah, tell that to a real estate agent."

He folded his arms. "You know, I could help out. Painting, or whatever else."

The thought of asking him to hook up the new light fixture crossed her mind, but she shook it away. He was swamped with his own job. "In all your spare time?"

He winced. "Yeah, you and me both."

Lori set a hand on her hip. "So, can I help you find anything? Want to decorate your trailer? Pick up some candy for trick-or-treaters?"

"No . . ." He glanced around again, then licked his lips.

Was he . . . nervous?

When his gaze landed on hers, she had the sudden urge to push up the brim of his ball cap to better see his eyes.

"I wanted to ask . . ." He exhaled. "To ask if you're available tomorrow night to go to a gala thing with me. It wouldn't be a date. I mean, you would be my date, but not like a date-date."

Lori stared at him. What was he talking about? "What kind of gala?"

"Oh. Yeah." He stuffed his hands into the pockets of his jeans. "Our company is getting some industry award and, uh, we're all going. Me, my brother and his wife, and her sister Penny. I thought . . ."

Lori waited.

He cleared his throat. "Sorry. This is kind of awkward and embarrassing, but Penny is, um, very assertive in her interest toward me. Bronson thinks it's all a riot, so he's no help. If I show up without a date to this gala, and there's drinking and dancing . . ." His voice trailed off again.

"Penny will be all over you?"

His face flushed, and Lori wanted to laugh. She didn't though. She'd never imagined that this sturdy, confident man could be cowed by a flirtatious sister-in-law.

Lori folded her arms. "Why don't you just tell her you're not interested?"

He moved one of his hands to his neck and rubbed the back of it. "It's not that simple. I mean, it should be that simple, and I've told her in the most casual ways I can think of. I can't be rude or hurt her feelings—directly, that is—because she has kind of a history."

This caught Lori's attention. Well, everything he was talking about had her full attention. "Like what?"

"She's one of those women who goes a little bananas if she doesn't get her way," he said, his voice quieting as if someone might overhear. "She keyed one of her ex's cars. She also destroyed the cell phone of another ex. But that's not what I'm worried about—some minor property damage. I don't want to mess up the dynamics of our company. At least not yet."

"So you need her to like you, but not stalk you?"

Malcom laughed, some of the tension leaving him. "Something like that."

Lori frowned though. "What do you mean—*not yet.*"

He rested both of his hands on the counter. "I've been thinking about breaking out of the company and doing my own thing. It's been a great ride and everything, and I'm grateful for the chance to work with my brother." His gaze fell. "There are some things though—red flags, maybe—and as soon as this condo project wraps up, I'm going to tell my brother that I'm setting out on my own."

"Red flags? Like what?" Lori lifted a hand. "Never mind. I don't mean to be so nosy."

He gazed at her for a moment, as if battling over how much to say. "Mostly financial stuff. I haven't gone so far as to request an audit though. When I look at the numbers, it all appears to be legit. But Bronson owns multiple homes. How does he pay for all of them? We're on the same salary. Even with his wife helping out part-time, none of us are millionaires."

Lori didn't know how to answer, and she wouldn't be able to understand the complications of his business. "Brandy is an accountant," she said. "You know, if you want someone to look at the numbers off the record."

Malcom's brows shot up. "Do you think she'd do it? I mean, off the record?"

"Probably," Lori said, although she wasn't expecting him to jump all over her suggestion. "She thinks you're pretty great. I mean, despite the fact that you haven't proposed to me."

His smile appeared. "It would be amazing if she agreed. I mean, I hope there's nothing to find, but peace of mind would be nice."

"I'm sure." The store phone rang, but Lori sent it to voicemail.

"Do you need to get that?"

"No, I'll call back if they leave a message."

Malcom nodded. "So, about the gala. What do you think?"

"It's tomorrow night?"

"Yeah, I'd pick you up around six, and then the thing will probably be a couple of hours." He paused, his smile tentative, his eyes hopeful. "The food should be decent, if nothing else."

She smiled, liking how he was acting all nervous again. "What's the dress code?"

"Uh, black tie?"

"You sound uncertain."

"We can go more casual if you want," he said, shifting his stance. "I know this is last minute. If you have to buy something, I'll pay."

She stared at him. "You'd buy me a formal dress just to get Penny out of your hair?"

He gave her a sheepish look. "Yeah. I mean, how much do those formals cost?"

"There's a wide range." Lori laughed. "Don't worry. I have something that will work. It's black, simple, but floor length."

"Sounds perfect to me," Malcom said, relief evident in his voice. "And I wouldn't expect any color other than black."

Lori just smiled at him. She kind of liked his teasing.

He rested his elbows on the counter, leaning closer. "And the earrings? Will they be Halloween-themed?"

"Is it October?"

He grinned and straightened. "Thanks so much, Lori. I mean it. I'll see you tomorrow night, then?"

"Yeah." She knew this wasn't him really asking her out, but her pulse was celebrating anyway.

"Okay, great." He tapped the counter, then hesitated. "Should we swap numbers? I mean, in case something comes up?"

It was all in innocence and, of course, smart. "Sure." After they exchanged numbers, Lori watched him walk out of the store. She had to tear her gaze away before he reached the sidewalk though, the door swinging shut behind him—just in case he looked back. She didn't want to be caught staring after him.

For the next twenty-four hours, it was all she could think about—going to the gala with Malcom. By Saturday afternoon, her stomach had tied itself into knots. She couldn't even finish the lunch she'd ordered in.

Feeling better, Marci said she'd do the closing so Lori could head upstairs to get ready around five p.m. Lori had told her she was going with a friend to a gala, not mentioning it was a male friend. Marci would figure it out soon enough, but Lori didn't want to risk any gossip happening because then her friend group would find out. And no, she hadn't said anything to them yet. She'd tell them after. When she had answers to the millions of questions they'd ask.

Five p.m. seemed to take forever to arrive, but when it did, Lori realized she needed more time to get ready. She'd underestimated the state of her hair, and it really needed to be washed. That would add on time that Lori didn't really have. Should she text Malcom that she'd be late? Or could she rush through everything else?

In the end, she didn't text him advance warning, but at 5:55 p.m. she finally pulled out her phone. *I'm going to need ten more minutes. When I see your truck, I'll come down. This is Lori, btw.*

His reply came a few seconds later. *No problem. This is Malcom, btw.*

Lori laughed, but it was more of a shaky laugh. And it wasn't ten minutes more. It was more like twenty minutes.

She could see Malcom waiting in his truck in front of the shop. Patiently. He hadn't even texted to ask if she was ready yet.

One last check in the mirror, and Lori decided everything was as good as it would get. She'd curled waves into her normally straight hair, and added more makeup than she usually wore. She'd hesitated over her earring choice, but finally settled on small silver pumpkins. Someone would have to look closely to determine what they actually were.

Finally, she couldn't delay any longer, and she headed down the stairs, holding one side of her gown up, balancing on her black heeled shoes. That was the only thing she'd probably regret tonight—choosing the shoes that might look the best with the dress, but would certainly hurt her feet if she was on them too much.

"Wow," Marci said as Lori entered the shop. "You look amazing. And you didn't tell me your friend was the builder."

Lori only smiled. "Thanks for closing up. Let me know if there are any issues. Otherwise, I'll see you Monday."

Marci's brows skyrocketed. "Um, I won't be able to wait that long for a report on your evening."

"We're going as friends, that's all. This is more of a favor, you know. A plus one to some awards gala."

Marci didn't look convinced, but she waved a hand. "Better hurry. Prince Charming has been trapped in his truck for like twenty minutes."

Lori's heart skipped a beat, and she glanced at the clock. So it had been nineteen minutes . . . nineteen minutes past her ten-minute grace period. Well, there was nothing to be done now.

She headed out of the shop, and before she could reach the passenger side, Malcom had climbed out of the truck and walked around the front. Lori had known he'd look great in a tuxedo, but wow. She'd have to remember to keep her eyes on his face. He opened the door for her, his gaze trained on her.

"Nice earrings."

Lori couldn't help it—she laughed. "Thanks. And nice tux. You clean up well."

The edge of his mouth lifted. "Thanks, and you look beautiful. Your dress is nice too."

A sigh rippled through Lori, and she moved to climb into the seat. It was a bit too high for her fitted dress. Malcom grasped her hand and helped her inside.

"It's going to be hard pretending this isn't a real date," he said, his voice low.

Before she could answer, he shut the door. What had he meant? That he *wanted* this to be a real date? No, she told herself. She couldn't let her mind go there.

# Eight

Lori looked stunning, in Malcom's opinion, but that wasn't what had his thoughts jumbled. This morning he'd reached out to Ian, who'd talked to Brandy, and she'd agreed to look at the financials for his company. "Give me a couple of days," she'd said.

So did that mean she might have some results by tomorrow night? Or the next night? It was one thing to wonder and worry on his own, but if Brandy came back with things that he couldn't brush off . . . then what? Confronting his brother on anything never turned out well. He'd learned that lesson in high school.

"The light's green," Lori said.

Malcom blinked. "Sorry." He pressed on the gas and continued through the intersection.

"I'm already a terrible date." He glanced over at her. "Did I tell you that you look beautiful?"

She smiled. "You did. But that compliment always makes me suspicious."

"How so?"

"Do I only look beautiful if I put on a formal dress and pile on the makeup?" she teased.

He winced. "That's not how I meant the compliment at all, but I see what you're saying. How about I tell you that you looked beautiful when I first met you. And you look equally beautiful now?"

Lori laughed, but her cheeks had flushed. "You're pretty good at flirting when you put your mind to it. I guess we should practice before I meet Penny?"

Malcom slowed at the next light. It seemed he was hitting every red light in town. "I'm not flirting . . . yet. Just being honest. And yeah, we need to talk about Penny."

"Is that what has you a million miles away?" she asked.

Malcom sighed. "Not exactly." The light turned green, and this time he didn't need any prompting. "Brandy agreed to look over my company's financials."

"Oh. Wow. That's great."

"Yeah." He accelerated and took the next turn leading to the highway.

"You don't sound too excited about it," Lori said.

"I guess I'm nervous about what she'll find."

"Because then you'll have to do something about it?"

"Exactly." Malcom checked his blind spot and merged onto the highway. "If she finds something, I can't just pretend it's my own paranoia."

"But then you'll know," Lori said. "And what you choose to do at that point is up to you. Having the information will be what you need to make the best-informed decision about your next steps."

"True." She was right, absolutely right.

Lori reached over and squeezed his arm. "It will be better to know than not to know. It will stop eating you up inside."

"You're right," he said. "You're beautiful and wise."

Lori laughed. "Okay, don't overdo the compliments. Without all my wise advice, you'd come to the same conclusion all on your own. You're just emotionally invested and I'm not, so it's easier for me to cut through all the other stuff."

"Like I said, wise."

She smirked. "So . . . what's our plan for Penny? How are we going to pull this all off?"

Malcom took the next exit and slowed for the light. "Great questions. She'll know that we've recently met—at least since the condo project started."

"Right. So we aren't too far into our dating relationship?"

"Exactly."

"Which means she'll be watching to see if we're affectionate."

"Likely." Malcom turned onto the road leading to the hotel where the gala was being held. He stole a glance at her. Yep. She looked beautiful. Tonight, and every time he'd seen her. "We can't be completely hands off, but we can't be kissing every minute either. Too much."

"Um, you didn't say this date would include kissing."

"It won't," Malcom rushed out, his heart lurching. What had he said? "I meant—"

Lori laughed. "You should see your face."

He blew out a breath, his stomach in knots. "I mean, I could step it up if needed." He pulled into the hotel parking lot and drove to the front doors, where a valet waited.

"I don't think so, Romeo," she said with another laugh. "Penny wouldn't buy it. Well, maybe she would, but it would feel over the top."

Malcom stopped the truck and looked over at her before climbing out. He wouldn't mind kissing her, but if he ever did, it wouldn't be for public display. And not in front of Penny. This wasn't anything he could confess to Lori, though. "I think plenty of flirting and some hand-holding would be perfect."

Lori's eyes were bright with amusement. "Okay."

He exhaled, trying to steady the nerves that kept zapping him. "Okay. And thanks again for all of this."

"Like you said, the food will probably be great."

Malcom laughed. Maybe this evening would be better than he expected. Maybe having Lori with him would keep Penny at arm's length and the crushing worry about his brother at bay. He climbed out of the truck, greeted the valet, then walked around to open her door.

He held out his hand to help her down, and her fingers grasped his. It was easy enough from there to just keep holding her hand, so he did. It fit neatly into his, and he decided that his thudding heart was from the event as a whole, and not just a simple touch from Lori.

"There you are." Bronson's voice sounded from across the lobby area. He wore a tuxedo as well. He stood about six inches shorter than Malcom, and his eyes were a pale blue like his mother's. "I wasn't sure if you'd already arrived. You didn't answer my texts."

"I was driving," Malcom said, keeping his tone even and light. Irritation already prickled his skin. Was his stepbrother really embezzling from the company? Was his wife, who stood next to him in a flowy multicolored dress, spending money left and right? She'd always seemed so conservative compared to her sister, but maybe she spent her money differently. Right now, she wore small diamond earrings and a small diamond pendant. Classy but expensive?

"Who do we have here?" Bronson's gaze landed on Lori.

"This is Lori. Lori, this is my brother Bronson and his wife Kari."

"Great to meet you," Bronson said, stretching out his hand, his curious gaze sweeping over her from head to foot. "I didn't know you were bringing a date."

"The invitation said to bring a plus one," Malcom said, again fighting to keep the irritation out of his tone.

Before Bronson could answer, Kari said to Lori, "You look so familiar. What's your last name?"

"Harding," she said, releasing Bronson's hand, then turning to Kari.

"Oh, that doesn't sound familiar," Kari continued. "Where are you from?"

"Everly Falls."

"Oh." Kari laughed.

Had her laugh been fake? Malcom wondered. He'd never thought anything about her was fake. So this was a new observation for him.

"Are you friends with Penny?" Kari continued with a bright smile.

Definitely a fake smile. What was going on?

"Who's Penny?" Lori asked, her tone curious and sweet at the same time.

Malcom wanted to tug her close and kiss her right then and there just for saying that.

Kari's brows shot up. "My sister. She and Malcom are really close, so I thought a friend of his would be a friend of hers too."

Lori looked up at Malcom, her gaze wide and innocent. "Why haven't you told me about Penny?"

"I guess because we've had so many other things to talk about." He felt Bronson's sharp gaze, and Kari's suspicious one. Malcom had to do something here . . . He slipped his arm about Lori's waist and drew her close. "You'll meet her tonight—she's great."

"Oh, I can't wait," Lori said, possessively placing a hand on his chest.

If he didn't know this was fake flirting, he would have been totally convinced.

"Speaking of Penny," Bronson cut in, "she's inside the ballroom, saving us a table."

"Excellent," Malcom said, sliding his hand away from Lori's waist and grasping her hand again. He felt Kari tracking every movement. Maybe the person they had to convince was her, not Penny.

And now Malcom was annoyed again. He'd brought up his concerns about Penny more than once to his brother, who had always laughed them off. But now it seemed like Kari was invested, which meant that Bronson knew exactly what was going on.

As they followed Bronson and Kari into the ballroom, Lori leaned close and whispered, "Smooth moves, Romeo."

He grinned down at her. "Right back at you, Juliet."

She returned his smile, and Malcom realized that despite all the irritants bombarding him, tonight might be fun. With Lori. Flirting with her—and yeah, holding her hand—was completely and undeniably enjoyable.

He tugged his gaze from hers, if only to not trip on his own feet, and spotted Penny. She was waving at them, a smile plastered on her face. Her eyes had already zeroed in on the woman at his side.

"Oh boy," Lori said under her breath. "I think I see Maleficent."

Malcom chuckled. "She's definitely noticing you." He liked the way Lori's fingers tightened around his.

Penny had gone all out, of course, wearing a dark yellow dress covered in sequins. Her blonde hair was piled on top of her head, complete with dangling earrings that looked like they were dripping with diamonds. Probably fake diamonds? Otherwise those earrings would cost thousands. Although Penny had a good salary as operations manager, it wasn't extravagant.

"Malc," Penny said as soon as they neared the table. She stepped close and kissed him on the cheek, lingering much longer than necessary. He couldn't remember when she'd ever kissed him on the cheek, so that was a new development. Wasn't bringing a date to this gala a deterrent for that?

"Hi, Penny," Malcom said, moving a step back from her, still holding Lori's hand. "This is Lori. Lori, this is Penny."

Lori stuck out her free hand. "Nice to meet you, Penny."

Penny glanced at her hand but didn't extend her own. "Nice to meet you too." Her expression tightened, then she looked over at her sister. "I told the waiters about your allergies, so they should come up with something you can eat."

"Oh thanks," Kari said, holding her sister's gaze as if trying to teleport some information.

Penny turned back to Malcom with a tight smile. "You can sit here, Malc." She motioned to a free chair between Kari and what looked to be Penny's seat, since a small purse sat at the place setting. "I didn't account for you bringing a friend, but there's a place by Bronson. Otherwise, the other seats are saved by someone else."

Penny was smooth, he'd give her that. "I'll be sitting by my *date*," he said. "You won't mind sitting by Bronson, will you?"

Her smile remained, but her eyes grew stormy. Malcom merely smiled back, then led Lori to the other side of the table. "Here's your purse," he said, picking it up and handing it over.

Penny practically snatched the purse away and strode over to where Bronson had seated himself.

Malcom pulled out the chair for Lori, and once she was seated, he sat down as well. "Is this the menu?" he asked, picking up the printed paper from the dinner plate in front of him. He felt the heat of Penny's gaze, but refused to meet it.

Lori nudged him. "Malc, huh?" she said in a quiet voice.

"Not my nickname," he said, turning his head. "Mac is okay, but not Malc."

Lori raised the water glass to her lips. "Noted."

He smiled, and she smiled back, then took a sip.

It was hard to look away from her, so he didn't. Openly staring at his date was acceptable, right? "Good water?"

Lori laughed. "Excellent."

Malcom was grateful for the music playing overhead, and the general hubbub of the room, so he could talk to Lori without everyone overhearing. He picked up his own water glass.

"You know, she's really pretty," Lori murmured. "I wouldn't blame you if you decided to ditch me for her."

"You're kidding, right?" Malcom said, and was happy to see Lori's smile appear. "I'll take real over fake any day."

Her smile widened. "Are you flirting now, Romeo?"

He set his arm around the back of her chair and leaned in close to whisper in her ear. "No, I was speaking the truth just now, but this . . ." He brushed her shoulder with his fingers. "This is flirting. What do you think?"

Lori shifted slightly so they were face to face, only a few inches apart. "I think . . . you're very skilled, Malc."

He groaned. "You did not just say that."

Her pretty smile appeared. "I did."

"I'll let one slip past, but after this, you'll be in trouble."

Her brows lifted. "What does that entail?"

He smirked. "Uh, I could drag you out of here and make you miss dinner."

"*Drag me?* I'm stronger than I look."

His gaze dipped to her mouth. "I could kiss you senseless, so you forget all about any nicknames."

"Remember we agreed on no kissing?"

It was true, but she was leaning quite cozily against him, and he didn't mind at all. "Right." He dragged in a breath and gave her a little space. "Maybe we should dance. Take a break from our audience."

Lori peeked at them from the corner of her eye. "No one else is dancing. Maybe after dinner?"

"That works too."

Three others arrived at their table and took their seats. Introductions were made all around. A man named Doug said he ran a water heater company, and the conversation springboarded from there, although Malcom barely remembered what anyone else said.

A waiter approached their table and took drink orders. By the time he left, a conversation had started between Doug and Penny. He was asking her questions about their business.

"Bronson is the magic behind everything," she gushed. "He's really the renaissance man, the idea man. As operations manager, I just keep up with him. And my sister Kari is a whiz at marketing and community outreach."

Doug seemed enthralled.

"Malcom over there is the boots-on-the-ground guy," she said. "He knows how to keep employees happy, which is so important. He has a kind heart and good listening skills."

All the words coming out of Penny's mouth were compliments, but they didn't feel like it. They felt like the praise someone would give a kid in school.

"Congratulations on your award tonight," Doug continued, smoothing down his comb-over. "Construction company of the year—really impressive."

"Thanks," Penny said, apparently the spokesperson tonight. "We should exchange information. I'd love to talk to you about your water heaters."

Malcom glanced at Bronson, but his brother didn't say anything.

"We have a five-year contract with another water-heater company," Malcom finally said. "Which we signed last year."

Penny shrugged. "Contracts can be broken if they aren't upheld."

He stared at her. "What's not being upheld?"

She merely smiled. "We can talk business later. Tonight is about celebrating and enjoying ourselves? Right, Lori?"

Lori lifted her chin. "I'm planning on it."

Penny laughed, a little too loud. "I like her, Malc. Where did you two meet?"

# Nine

LORI SHOULDN'T HAVE BEEN SURPRISED at the barrage of questions Penny threw at Malcom. She *was* surprised, though, at the way a grown woman was acting so ridiculous, because some of what she said was completely intrusive.

"He's a workaholic, Lori," Penny said, as her wineglass was filled for the second time. "Both brothers are. My sister had to retrain her husband to even take a vacation."

Bronson chuckled and lifted his glass in a mock toast. "And look at me now. I don't even have my phone on me tonight."

Penny grinned. "You're such an inspiration." In the next second, she was practically glowering at Lori. "Now, what is it *you* do?"

Lori had already told her once. Was this some sort of strategy to intimidate her?

"She owns the shop across from the worksite, as she already told you," Malcom said. "Now, anyone hungry? This looks good."

"You're already letting him speak for you?" Penny asked, laughing as if she was trying to make it seem she was being funny.

Lori gave her a tight smile and turned her attention to her plate. The chicken parmesan and asparagus did look great. She took a bite.

"What do you think?" Malcom asked.

"About the food or . . ."

"The food," he said with a chuckle. Then he sobered. "Sorry about all the questions. I think Penny has outdone herself."

Lori set her hand over his and squeezed, mostly for Penny's benefit. She was watching them from across the table. "So it's all smooth sailing from here?"

Malcom's eyes crinkled at the corners. "If only we could be so lucky."

They continued to eat and chat, and eventually Penny's focus shifted once again to Doug. It didn't take too much analysis to see that the way she was speaking about the company was bothering Malcom. Did they not have management meetings to get on the same page with each other?

The MC tapped the microphone, then began to speak at the podium in front of the room, and for the next thirty minutes, awards and accolades were announced. Bronson, Malcom, Penny, and Kari all went to the front of the room to receive their award. A photographer stopped them on the way back for pictures, and Penny wedged herself right next to Malcom.

Lori had to force herself not to laugh at his expression. He was truly uncomfortable, and it wasn't funny. Well, only a little funny. Regardless, she was glad she could come tonight and help him out. She couldn't remember a time when a non-date had actually been so fun, let alone a real date.

Lori ate a couple bites of dessert—raspberry cheesecake—as she waited for Malcom to return. Penny held on to his arm, drilling him with questions, her smile tight.

Malcom's shoulders were tense, and he looked like he'd rather be anywhere else than talking to her.

Lori looked over at Bronson, who'd just returned to the table and sat down with Kari. They set the glass trophy between their place settings, admiring it. Didn't Bronson see what was going on with his stepbrother? How bothered Malcom was? Did he not care?

Not that Lori was a family-dynamic expert. She didn't have any siblings—let alone jealous or vindictive ones. Because Lori had decided that Bronson must be one or the other, or even both. Were high school sports really so important as to divide two brothers?

"Hey," Malcom said, standing next to her. "Want to go check out the silent auction?"

Lori stood immediately. "Sure."

He grasped her hand, leading her to the row of tables where a few people milled about, putting in their bids while the MC continued with the program.

"Congrats on your award," she said.

Malcom nodded.

"Looks like you got some good photos," she continued.

He looked at her then, his expression amused. "Depends on your standard for good photos."

Lori smiled, and his mouth lifted. At least this was something he could smile about. "Was she so awful?"

"Worse." He squeezed her hand. "Have I thanked you for coming?"

"You have."

They continued browsing the auction items. "Spa day for two?" she teased.

"Sign us up."

"It would mean a second date, or a second non-date."

Malcom picked up the pen and wrote down both of their

names on the next line, then he put in parenthesis: *Call me at this number . . .*

"We're not staying all night?"

He chuckled. "We can if you want."

Lori glanced over at the table with his brother and the others. Penny hadn't touched her dessert, and although she seemed to be talking to her sister, her eyes were definitely on Malcom.

"Not unless there's second dessert."

"Now you're talking," he said in a low voice. "I like a woman who doesn't skip dessert."

Lori raised her brows. "Now whose standards are low?"

He only grinned.

Applause broke out for the end of whatever the MC had said, and the music started again. They continued down the line of tables, and Malcom signed up for two more things. Lori bid on a book basket.

"We should dance," Malcom said. "You know, solidify our date, then get out of here."

"You're *so* romantic," she said with a laugh.

He led her to the dance floor, where a few other couples had started dancing.

"Is she watching us?" Lori asked as she moved into his arms.

His hold was loose, one hand resting lightly at her waist, the other hand clasping hers.

"I don't know," he said. "Probably."

Lori kind of liked that his eyes were trained on her. "What was she asking when you walked back from the stage?"

"Oh." Malcom blinked. "She wanted to know how long we'd been seeing each other."

"What did you tell her?"

"Three weeks—because that's technically true. We met

three weeks ago. She also said it was cute to see me in a fling. Then she said that if I wanted to have a more substantial date, I should have invited her. I pointed out that she was already invited. To which she said that she could tell you weren't all that interested in me—and were probably in it for the free meal."

Lori scoffed. "Wow, I don't know if I should be offended or impressed. She totally nailed it. You did promise a good meal."

"I did." Malcom's smile made her pulse jump around, or maybe it was how he pulled her a little closer.

He also slowed his movements, just a tad slower than the beat of the song. "How's the dancing? Is it better than you expected?"

Lori laughed. "You're a passable dancer. And you smell nice. Cologne?"

"Just my shower wash. You're so full of compliments. I like it," he teased. He drew her closer again, and she couldn't help but close her eyes and relax into him with a smile.

His subtle scent was nice, and his arm around her was nice, and the bristle along his jaw was nice . . . well, everything about him was nice.

When the song ended and switched to a faster tune, Lori felt reluctant to stop dancing, even though her high heels were starting to pinch. She opened her eyes to find Malcom's gaze intent on her.

"You totally had me convinced," he said in that deep voice of his.

"About what?" she asked.

"That you're actually enjoying this date—and not just because of the food."

Lori tilted her head. "What's not to enjoy? Even with Penny in the equation, you're a good date—I mean, a good dancer. Because this isn't a real date."

Malcom just gazed at her for a few more seconds, not saying anything.

It wasn't fair that he was so effortlessly handsome. His hazel eyes were mostly brown tonight, and dark stubble peppered his chin and jaw. Lori couldn't really blame Penny for her obsession with him.

"Maybe we could hang out sometime, *without* my family as an audience," Malcom said.

Lori's heart thumped. "What did you have in mind?"

"You need to screen it beforehand?" he asked, his dimples appearing.

It wasn't lost on her that she was still standing in his arms as the dancers moved around them. Both of his hands were at her waist as she rested her hands on his biceps. "Prescreening is a must for me."

"Fair enough, I'll come up with something you won't be able to turn down."

He released her then and slid a hand into hers. They walked back to the table to say their goodbyes, and Lori felt like she was walking an inch above the ground. Had Malcom just asked her out? Malcom had asked her out. Officially. Yeah, as friends, but there would be no trying to act fake around anyone.

Before they left the table, Penny said, "It was nice meeting you, Lori. Probably won't see you again, so good luck with your little shop."

Lori could only hope she wouldn't see Penny again, but that would mean that she wouldn't be around Malcom much, so she didn't want to hope for that. "Good luck to you too," she said with a wide smile.

Confusion marred Penny's eyes, but her smile turned Cheshire.

Lori had never felt the need to compete over a man until tonight. It was ridiculous really, but Penny was bringing out the ridiculous in her. And Lori didn't even know the woman, not really. Thankfully, they were leaving, and she could have Malcom all to herself. Well, not like *that*, but just being away from Penny would be great. For his sake, of course.

As they waited outside for the valet to bring Malcom's truck, she thought he'd release her hand. But he didn't, and Lori found that she didn't mind.

Might as well see it through to the very end.

Again, he helped her into the truck, then he shrugged out of his jacket and set it in the back seat before he climbed into the driver's side.

Lori slipped off her shoes to give her toes a break. "Do you think Penny bought it?"

Malcom pulled out of the parking lot. "I don't see how she couldn't. I mean, you're pretty fabulous, and I think I did a decent job too."

Lori laughed, even though a tiny part inside of her was aching. "You were fabulous too. Is she always so nasty, or was it just special treatment to me?"

"She's very . . . clingy toward me," Malcom said. "But I've never brought another woman around her, so this was a first."

"Hmm."

"But I believe we were convincing. Not only to Penny, but to my brother. He's already texted me, asking if we're serious."

"In only a couple of weeks?" Lori asked, surprised.

"He means . . . well, he's asking if we're sleeping together in not so many words."

"Oh." Lori bit her lip. "That's kind of bold—even for a brother to ask. Did you tell him it's none of his business?"

"I'm not answering, period." Malcom reached for her hand. "I'd never confess that sort of thing to him anyway. And even if this were a real date, I wouldn't want to mess things up by racing to the finish line."

Lori looked down at his hand holding hers. "Is that what the kids are calling it now?"

Malcom laughed and squeezed her hand. It felt like a squeeze to her heart.

"Your stepbrother seems nice enough, but I got kind of a strange vibe from him."

"What's that?" His voice was filled with worry.

"Like he's competing with you," Lori said. "I'm probably reading into things, just because of your concerns. So that might have biased me."

"Maybe, or maybe not."

They continued to drive in silence for several moments, and Lori wondered if his holding her hand was left over from their fake date, or if it was something more. He had asked her out—although there were currently no plans.

As they merged onto the highway, his thumb traced over her skin. "Is this okay?" he asked in a soft voice.

"Yes," she said, because it was, although she had some questions. "Are we still on a fake date?"

"It wasn't completely fake." He glanced over at her. "I like you, Lori. I mean, I know that I don't have time to date, and you don't want to date, but that doesn't change the fact that I like you."

Lori's heart felt like it had climbed into her throat. "I like you too," she said simply, "and I don't mind the hand-holding, but the other stuff . . . you know, that would be way beyond friends hanging out."

"The other stuff?" he asked. "Oh, you mean, like kissing?"

She had to laugh. "Yeah, kissing. That kind of stuff turns things into a relationship. Which neither of us wants."

"Right," Malcom said. "Good boundary."

"Can you live with it?" Lori teased.

"I'll try."

His low voice resonated through her, but she decided to ignore the racing of her pulse. Malcom would be moving on in a few months, and Lori wasn't going to follow after any man. She had her store, and she was happy with living in her small corner of life.

When Malcom came to a stop in front of her shop, he opened her door again. Then he walked her to the front door.

She unlocked it, then turned. "Thanks for dinner. And I hope the night was all it needed to be."

Malcom stood a couple of feet away, hands in his pockets, as the breeze ruffled his hair and shirt. "It was more. Thanks, Lori."

"No problem."

He stepped close and lifted a hand to her cheek, then he pressed a kiss on her other cheek. Before she could absorb what he was doing, he'd stepped back, restoring the space between them.

# Ten

It wasn't hard for Malcom to decide which text thread to respond to. The weekend had passed much too quickly. No word from Brandy yet on the financials. Plenty of texts had come in from Penny though—texts he was trying to ignore. But it was the texts from Lori that kept him smiling.

They were in a late-night debate of what they should do at their next "get-together." They'd decided it would be the night before Halloween since that's when their schedules aligned next. It felt like a long time away. But it was fine, Malcom had told himself, to miss her a little bit. That didn't stop him from glancing across the street about a hundred times a day. He'd seen her a couple of times, coming and going in her car.

Apparently she was a night owl too, and eleven p.m. wasn't too late to argue about their plans. She'd already ruled out hiking—a storm was coming in. And bowling—it was "battle of the leagues" this week.

*Movie?* he texted. *Your friend Everly told me the theater in town shows a mix of oldies and new releases. Your pick.*

*I'll look up what's showing,* she wrote back.

This was major progress for Malcom. Not that taking her

to a movie was his first choice since there'd be more staring at the screen than talking. And the point of hanging out was to get to know her better.

A text came in from Penny. There was no good reason for her to be texting him outside of work hours or about things that weren't work related. But he could tell it was a photo—with the message: *Thought you might like this*—and he was too curious not to click on it.

He opened the text to look at the photo. It was of him and Lori at the gala. Dancing, when she was leaning into him, her eyes closed. Malcom drew in a breath as the memories of that night rushed back. But then he wondered why *Penny* would take the photo.

Her next text arrived: *Someone from the gala took these and forwarded them to our office. Maybe this brings back good memories, or bad? Have you already dumped her? Wasn't sure if she was a one-night stand.*

Penny followed up the text with a winking emoji.

Malcom wanted to ignore the text, like he'd ignored most of her other ones this week that weren't work related. And he didn't want to get into a texting convo with her right now. But he also didn't want her accusing him of a one-night stand, not with anyone, especially Lori.

*We're still dating. Thanks for the pic,* he wrote.

Her reply came immediately. *Ooo. That's a record for you, right? Bronson is going to lose his bet.* Another winking emoji.

Malcom groaned. He didn't want to know the details about any bet, and he certainly wasn't going to ask Bronson about it. Or Penny. He didn't reply, but instead saved the photo to his phone, then forwarded it to Lori.

*We look cozy,* she replied. She didn't ask where the photo came from, and he didn't offer up the information. Frankly, he was tired of talking about Penny anyway.

Another text came through from Lori: *Dracula is showing at 8:00 p.m. Sounds perfect to me.*

Malcom laughed and texted back. *Really? Which version?*

*I'm impressed you know there are different versions. It's 1958, with Peter Cushing and Christopher Lee.*

*Excellent, what time should I pick you up? Dinner first?*

*7:30, and I'm planning on eating the overpriced food at the theater. Bring your credit card. Unless you want to go Dutch since this isn't a date?*

*I'm paying,* he wrote.

She sent a pumpkin emoji with heart eyes. He might have stared at it too long.

Malcom didn't know what it was about Halloween week, but it seemed the universe was conspiring against him. Rick came down with the flu, so Malcom had to fill in on maintenance several times at the cabin community, two of their suppliers had delivery delays, and Brandy emailed him early the day he was supposed to go to the movies with Lori and said they should meet ASAP.

She was coming into town anyway that day, so what time worked?

*Anytime,* Malcom had texted. *I'll make myself available.*

By the time she arrived at his trailer, he had been pacing so much, he felt like a zoo animal. He put up a sign on the door of the trailer that said, "Manager off site, call this number for emergencies," then hoped there'd be no phone calls.

Brandy was her usual bubbly self, but Malcom immediately sensed that the news she had to deliver wouldn't be good. Otherwise, why not talk over the phone or through email?

He invited her to sit at the single desk, and pulled over another chair so they could both look at the laptop screen, where he'd opened up the spreadsheets he'd sent to her.

Brandy grasped the mouse and moved the curser to the

top of the first one. "Now, I want you to pay attention to the numbers in this column. You don't need to memorize them, but look at the pattern. It stands out."

Malcom gazed at the column she'd highlighted. It was the accounts receivable column, and the numbers were all increasing in order, by ten dollars each. It was kind of odd. "Maybe those are estimates?"

"I compared this column to the invoices on file, and they all match the invoice number." Brandy clicked to another spreadsheet and highlighted one of the columns.

Malcom didn't need to ask her to go back to the first spreadsheet to see that the numbers were an exact replica, although the listed items varied.

"What is this?" His stomach had tightened. "What am I looking at?"

"Duplicated numbers and duplicated invoices, except the item and the date has changed." Brandy clicked on another spreadsheet. "Two years in a row might be a coincidence, but it's a long shot. And a third year? Here's last year's accounts receivable report."

The numbers in the column were duplicates again—or triplicates, he supposed. "Is this a mistake? Lazy accounting?"

"A mistake would be very generous. And lazy accounting might happen, but this feels deliberate. The accounts receivable are the same each year, yet the expenses keep increasing, which means that your company should be operating at a loss. At least that's what's being reported to the Internal Revenue Service."

Malcom rubbed at his forehead. "So this creative accounting saves us on taxes?"

"Yep." Brandy released a breath. "I mean, it might eventually be caught, and you'll be fined and ordered to pay back taxes. But that's not what I'm most worried about."

He dropped his hand. "There's more?"

Brandy clicked over to the next spreadsheet. "This is showing payroll by month."

He nodded. The numbers all looked normal.

"Yet..." She scrolled to the far right on the spreadsheet, advancing through columns Malcom hadn't noticed before. "This column shows transfers to another account. I don't have access to any of these accounts, so I can't verify them. But I'm thinking once you log into the payroll account, you'll see extra transactions that aren't going to payroll."

Malcom frowned and pulled up the banking app on his phone. He opened the business account and scrolled through the recent withdrawals. There were a lot of them because of all the employees in the company. It would take him forever to compare the withdrawals to payroll.

"Let me log into the bank on the laptop," he said.

Brandy scooted over, and he sat in front of the laptop and entered in his password information. As he scrolled through the dozens of transactions, she said, "Look for amounts that are outside of payday. See where all of these payments are coming out on the first and the fifteenth of the month? Look for anything on other days."

Malcom paused on a payment that came out a few days ago on the twenty-sixth in the amount of $3,300. It looked pretty innocent since it wasn't a huge amount and several people in the company made that amount twice a month. Just the date was suspicious. Then he looked at the twenty-fifth and saw another amount of $3,300. In fact, that same amount had been deducted multiple times a month outside of payroll dates.

"Where's the money going?" he asked as he clicked on the transaction to find out more information. It only had another routing number attached, but no account number, of course.

"It's going to another bank, but it's not a direct deposit transaction," Brandy said. "It's a manual transfer. Open a couple of the others and see if they're the same time of day."

Malcom did so, but they were all different times of the day. He exhaled, his skin prickling. "Payroll is going out to someone in the company who I don't know about."

Brandy nodded. "There might be more. But after finding these two issues, I thought it would be a decent place to start."

Malcom downloaded the most recent bank statement and saved the PDF to the hard drive. "What do you think I should do?"

"I think you have a few choices," Brandy said. "I talked to Austin about this in very broad terms—I didn't even mention your name. He once owned a successful company, something to do with data storage. But things with his business partner went south. He recommended hiring a lawyer."

Malcom felt like he'd been slapped in the face. "That seems extreme. This is my brother and my in-laws."

"I agree," Brandy said. "Family's important. There might be a good explanation, or like you said, lazy accounting. But if there's fraud, or other things, then you'll be liable as part-owner of the company."

Malcom pushed to his feet and paced the small area. His head pounded, and his mouth tasted bitter. He'd been suspicious for a while, but this . . . this shone a spotlight on everything. Was it Bronson? Or was he in on it with his wife? Was it Penny? Was it all three of them?

No one else in the company had access to their accounts.

"I need to talk to my brother," Malcom said, stopping to face Brandy. "I don't know if he'll tell me the truth, but I need to at least have the conversation before I can decide what to do next."

As soon as Brandy left, he called Bronson. The call went

to voicemail, so Malcom left a message, then texted his brother that they needed to meet right away.

Then, because he felt like he might literally go crazy, and he needed to talk this through with someone, he called Lori. The minute she answered, he wondered if he'd made a mistake. It was the middle of the workday for her, and she was probably busy.

"Hey, it's Malcom."

"Yeah, I know," she teased, her voice light. "Don't tell me you're bailing on tonight."

"What? No." Malcom tried to focus on what she was saying. "I do need to talk to you though. Brandy was just here."

"Brandy?" she echoed. "Oh, you mean about the financial statements you had her look at?"

"Yeah," he said quietly.

"Sounds like the news isn't good," Lori said in a softer tone. "What's going on?"

"Uh . . ." He rubbed the back of his neck. "Are you swamped? I wondered if we could talk in person. I'm waiting for Bronson to call me back. I might have to track him down if he doesn't respond soon."

"Sure, are you at your trailer?" Lori asked. "I can come over there and have Marci watch the place. We aren't busy anyway on account of the rain."

Malcom hadn't even noticed it had started to rain. He moved to the window, where raindrops pattered against the pane. "That would be great. Thanks, Lori."

He hung up and literally watched through the window for her. Moments later, she came out of the shop and opened an umbrella. She crossed the street after checking for traffic, then hurried across the parking lot.

He opened the trailer door as she neared. She was wearing a flowy black dress with black boots that hit just below her knees. Her earrings of choice were white ghosts. Any other day, he might have teased her about them. Not today.

"Thanks for this," he said, and motioned for her to come inside. After she set the umbrella aside, he offered her a chair.

It took him seconds to pull up the spreadsheets again on the laptop. He walked her through what Brandy had disclosed.

"Wow, I don't even know what to say," Lori said in a subdued tone. "This is really rotten of your brother, or whoever is responsible. I mean . . . there's been a lot of money hidden. I wonder how far back it goes?"

Malcom's shoulders sagged. "At least three years—which is what I gave to Brandy. We've only been in business for six, and despite this terrible news, I'd hate to think it's been going on the whole time."

"What are you going to do?" Lori asked. "I mean, what are you going to tell your brother?"

"I don't know." Malcom rubbed a hand down his face. "I hope he'll confess if it was him. I hope it's not him, of course. But I hope more lies don't happen." He folded his arms and focused on Lori. "I've been wanting to get out on my own anyway, like I told you, but I feel like I need to do it now."

Her brows lifted. "Like today?"

"This week at least."

She nodded. "You could set up an LLC online. Put in your resignation to your brother. Then get your name taken off of everything with him."

"Yeah." He googled small-business licenses and had just pulled up the online application when his phone rang. He froze when he saw it was Bronson.

"I can give you some privacy," Lori said, standing to leave.

"You can stay," Malcom said, picking up his phone. "Hey, Bronson, where are you? We need to meet."

Bronson's voice came through tinny. "No can do. I'm at the golf tournament, remember?"

Malcom remembered now. It was a two-day charity golf tournament that Bronson and Penny played in every year. It was usually toward the end of October, but this was the first year the second day would be on Halloween itself. It also meant that Bronson wouldn't be back in town until tomorrow night. He didn't want to bring up the financial stuff when Bronson was with Penny. They might team up and put together more lies.

"All right," Malcom said. "When do you get back home? We need to meet sooner than later."

"I'll be back around six o'clock tomorrow," Bronson said. "What's going on, man? What's the rush?"

"It can keep until tomorrow," Malcom said, trying to keep his voice nonchalant. "Have a good tournament." Then he hung up and looked over at Lori. He told her about the golf.

She nodded. "Kari doesn't play?"

He paused at this. "She does, but she doesn't like to compete."

Lori rubbed her hands over her knees. "Hey, if you need to cancel tonight, I'll understand."

The fact that she offered was sweet, but he didn't want to be alone with his circling thoughts tonight. "I think the distraction will be good for me."

# Eleven

THE *DRACULA* MOVIE WAS NEARLY over, and Malcolm's arm had been pressed against Lori's the whole time. She was pretty sure he didn't even realize it. And she also didn't think he was paying much attention to the movie. Oh, his eyes were open and on the screen, but he hadn't reacted to much of what was going on. Not that she could blame him, because he had a lot on his mind.

She'd wondered if he'd hold her hand again, but he hadn't. They had both once again reiterated that they were only hanging out as friends, so then why was her pulse jumping around at the slightest contact with him? He also smelled great—a subtle cologne and something like outdoorsy pine.

He wasn't wearing his standard ball cap and T-shirt and jeans, but instead wore navy slacks and a light-brown sweater, which made the gold in his hazel eyes seem to pop out. And she was pretty sure he hadn't shaved for a few days.

As the closing credits ran, Malcolm didn't make any move to leave. Which was fine with Lori, since she usually liked to read the credits. Not that she would recognize names, like Everly might. But it was interesting to see the scope of the numerous people who had a hand in creating a film.

She also didn't want to move for a minute, because she was kind of full from eating so much popcorn. It was Malcolm's fault, because he barely ate any, so Lori felt like she didn't want it to go to waste.

After the theater had emptied of everyone else, Malcolm shifted and looked over at her. "What did you think?" he asked. "Was it as good as you remembered it?"

"I loved it," Lori said. "But I think I was paying more attention to you than actually watching it."

His brows lifted. "Sorry about that. Was I distracting you?"

"You were." She squeezed his arm, then withdrew her hand. "I'm sorry you're dealing with so much. Maybe we should have gone on a run or something. Burned off your frustration."

"Do you run?" Curiosity entered his voice.

"No, but I've seen you out running." It might be a little embarrassing to admit, but if *Dracula* couldn't distract him, what could? "I mean, if you do want to go running, I can cheer you on."

Malcom smiled—probably his first genuine smile of the night. "Come on. Let's get out of here. I think we need a real meal somewhere."

Lori moved to her feet. "Everything's closed. You know, small town and all."

Malcom picked up the empty popcorn bucket. "I could cook—I've got some chicken, and I can make rice. Nothing fancy."

Lori hesitated. It was after ten p.m., and tomorrow would be crazy at the store with Halloween activities. A lot depended on the weather too. If the weather was decent, they'd have most of it outside, but if it was too cold or it rained, it would have to be moved inside the store.

"Or not," Malcom said with a gentle smile. "We could have cold cereal. Do you like Lucky Charms?"

Lori laughed. "I do, but you're probably exhausted."

He shrugged. "I'm getting my second wind," he said in a ridiculous *Dracula* accent.

"Just for that, I'll come over for a little bit," she said. "I never sleep much the night before Halloween anyway."

"That's right—you have your store event tomorrow," Malcom said as they walked out of the theater. "I can't wait to see your costume. You'll have to text me a photo since I'll probably be with Bronson trying to see if our company will survive."

They'd reached the truck, and Lori set a hand on his arm. "I'm sorry you have to deal with all of that. I guess since neither of us will be sleeping, we should cook."

"It's a deal." Malcom opened the door for her, and she climbed up into the truck.

The ride back to their neighborhood was quiet, but Lori didn't mind a man who didn't feel like he had to fill the silence all of the time. By the time they reached his trailer, a light rain had started.

Malcom opted for real food versus Lucky Charms, and Lori wandered about the trailer as he cooked. There was a lot more to the trailer than what it seemed on the outside. The main area doubled as a kitchen and an office. A door separated the next section, and through the partially opened door, she could see the outlines of a bedroom.

The kitchen area had a small table with two chairs. Everything was clean and tidy, which it had to be in such limited space. She paused to look at the handful of photos he'd posted on a white board. "Are these your parents?"

He looked over from where he was grilling the chicken in a fry pan. "Yeah, before the divorce. I was about six, I guess.

My mom is on her third marriage now to a guy named Phil. Really good guy, and I think this one will actually stick."

"And Bronson is from another marriage?"

"Exactly. My dad remarried and got Bronson as part of the package."

The next photo showed Malcom in a basketball team photo. A third was at a wedding—Bronson and Kari's. Another showed him and Bronson on what looked like a fishing trip. It was kind of charming he had these photos up.

"Did you hear that?" Malcom asked.

Lori looked over at him. She had to admit, he looked quite appealing standing at the narrow stove, making food for her. "Hear what?"

He brought a finger to his lips, and above the sound of the sizzling chicken, she heard a small cry. No, a whine . . . or . . . "I think it's a cat," she said.

"A cat?"

Lori headed to the door and opened it, Malcom right behind her. The rain had started up again, but she stepped out. Another meow sounded, this time more frantic.

"Where are you?" Lori said in a soft voice. "Are you getting wet?"

She crouched next to the trailer and looked under it. It was too dark to see much.

The cat meowed again, but it sounded like a kitten. She pulled out her phone from her pocket.

"Do you see anything?" Malcom asked, crouching next to her.

She turned on the flashlight and two glowing eyes popped into view. "Oh, it's a kitten." She handed the phone to him, then held out her hand to the kitten. "Come here, baby. It's okay. We'll get you warm."

"We will?" Malcom mused.

"Go get a piece of that chicken. She's probably starving."

Malcom stood and headed into the trailer. Seconds later, he was back with a piece of chicken.

"Hold it out to her, and then I'll grab her."

"What are we doing, Lori?"

"Catching a cat."

He chuckled and held out the piece of chicken.

The cat meowed and moved forward, its poor little body trembling. Lori couldn't make out the color since its fur was muddy. When it made a snatch for the chicken, she grabbed the kitten. Its tiny claws held on to the food, and the kitten chowed it down as Lori carried it into the trailer.

Malcom came in behind her and shut the door.

"Do you have a towel I can use to wipe her off?" she asked.

Malcom produced a towel, then brought over another piece of chicken. The kitten ate that one too, and as Lori toweled it off, it began to purr.

"Oh, it's adorable," she said. "But homeless." She looked up at Malcom. "You should adopt it. I think someone abandoned it here."

"You mean someone dropped it off here on purpose?" he asked. "Maybe it ran away? Maybe a family is looking for it?"

"I doubt it." Lori picked up the kitten and held its rumbling body against her. "She's pretty rough around the edges. Very skinny. She'll need a bath. Maybe tomorrow when she's not starving."

"I thought cats bathed themselves," he said, his expression dubious.

"They do, but this one needs extra help." Lori peeled the cat from where it clung to her clothing. "Maybe we can use a washcloth to get some of the mud off."

Malcom disappeared again, then returned with a washcloth. Lori turned on the kitchen sink and let the water run until it was warm. Then she began to clean the kitten. It kept squirming, so she spoke to it in a soothing tone. "You're okay. You're home now."

"Lori, I know nothing about cats," Malcom said. "Didn't you used to have a cat? I think this is your next one."

She looked up into his earnest face. "Didn't you have pets as a kid?"

"Bronson had a dog," Malcom said. "I'm not opposed to a cat, but this would be the worst place—a trailer on a construction site. Plus, most of my days are twelve hours at least. Don't you think she'd be better off with you?"

Lori looked down at the kitten. Now she could see that with some of the mud cleaned off, it was an orange tabby. "*Him*," she said. "This is a boy."

Malcom's brows rose. "I think he'd look cute in a Halloween costume, don't you?"

She smiled. "Maybe next year. This year, he's going to be resting."

Malcom reached out a finger and scratched the top of the kitten's head. "He's a tenacious little thing. Like a miniature tiger."

"Maybe we can call him Tiger?" Lori suggested.

"I think it's fitting." He took the washcloth and rinsed it out, then handed it back to her.

As she continued to work on cleaning the kitten, he finished preparing dinner. Tiger got a few more pieces of chicken and a bowl of water. Lori couldn't keep her eyes off of the adorable creature. The kitten explored the trailer, then climbed up her pant leg with its tiny claws. In minutes, it was sleeping on her lap.

"All right, it's settled," she said, her heart feeling like it might burst. "I'm taking him home with me. But first, I might be stuck on this chair all night. It's against the laws of nature to move if a cat is asleep on your lap."

Malcom's chuckle was low. "Should I get you a pillow and a blanket? I can turn the lights off too."

Lori grinned. "Would you?"

He rose as if to do just that, when the kitten's head lifted, and he meowed.

"Light sleeper," she said with a laugh.

Malcom began to clear the dishes from the kitchen table. "Is there a crate or something the kitten can sleep in, so it doesn't keep you up all night?"

"Oh, I don't mind," Lori said, stroking the soft fur. "He can just curl up next to me until he's comfortable at my place. Then I can train him to use the cat bed." Her voice hitched, and she swallowed back her emotion.

Malcom had started to rinse off the dishes, but he turned. "Are you sure this is all okay? I can take him to the animal shelter in the morning."

But Lori had already fallen in love. Unless the kitten had truly escaped a loving family, she considered Tiger hers. She kissed the top of his head. "I'm okay."

"Do you want to take some chicken with you?" he offered. "Or I can buy stuff in the morning for it."

Tomorrow would be extremely busy, and she didn't have a litter box or kitten food.

At her hesitation, Malcom said, "I really don't mind. I'm going to have a lot of nervous energy tomorrow anyway while I'm waiting until I can talk to Bronson in person. Why don't you text me a list, and I'll go to the pet store—is there a pet store in Everly Falls?"

"The local grocery store has everything," Lori said. She was trying to think if she'd ever been on such a unique date—or hanging-out event. Malcom was being really sweet and patient and accommodating about all of this. Especially considering he was in a world of hurt.

The kitten yawned and burrowed into her lap again. Lori's heart tugged with protectiveness. What sort of person would abandon a kitten? She had a sudden thought. What if there were more kittens out there?

"We need to see if there are more abandoned cats," she said.

Malcom turned from the sink, drying his hands on a towel. "More?"

"Yeah, maybe a whole litter was dropped off." Lori picked up the kitten and moved to her feet. "We should look."

He hesitated, then nodded. "Okay. I'll look. You stay here since it's still raining."

He pulled on a jacket, then grabbed a flashlight and headed outside. Lori paced the kitchen area with the sleeping kitten in her arms. Malcom took longer than she expected, and by the time he came back inside, his jacket and hair were damp with rain.

"I looked all over, under the trailer and throughout the parking lot. I didn't see anything, or hear any meowing, but maybe daylight will be better."

"Thanks for looking anyway," she said. A water droplet skated down the side of his face, and she wanted to brush it away for him. But she kept her hands to herself.

"No worries." He paused. "Should I drive you in my truck? I don't have an umbrella."

"It's fine, I can walk," Lori said.

Malcom nodded. "I'll walk you."

"There's no need for both of us to get wetter."

He opened the door and held it for her.

"Don't say you weren't warned," Lori teased.

Malcom chuckled and headed outside after her. They walked quickly across the lot, then crossed the empty street together.

The light over the shop's door glowed yellow. Thankfully, there was an awning too, so they were out of the rain while Lori fumbled for her shop keys. There was also a back entrance next to a second door to her apartment, but that would entail more rain.

"Here, I'll hold the cat," Malcom said.

Lori relinquished the kitten, who was awake again, and dug out the keys from her handbag. She opened the door, then turned to retrieve Tiger.

Malcom handed him over. "Do you need help with anything?" he asked. His eyes were hooded beneath the door light, and the dark night surrounding them only seemed to accentuate the breadth of his shoulders.

"No, I've got it for now." Lori smiled at him.

"I'll be waiting for your supply list." Malcom scratched the top of the kitten's head. Then his eyes lifted. "Thanks for tonight. It was the perfect distraction."

"You paid for the movie and snacks, then you cooked, and finally you rescued this kitten," she said. "I should be thanking you."

"We can both thank each other."

Lori laughed. She wanted to hug him, but would that be crossing a line? Besides, she was holding a cat. What was the protocol here?

Malcom took care of her debate though. He leaned down and kissed her cheek. "Good night, Lori."

# Twelve

MALCOM RARELY REMEMBERED HIS DREAMS, but he woke up in the middle of sprinting after his brother. Bronson had been running through the trees that bordered the condo complex. He awoke, feeling bothered that his brother had outrun him, even if it was only a dream. Bronson golfed, yes, and hiked, but Malcom knew that if there were ever a race between them, he'd win, hands down.

He gazed up at the ceiling. The sun wasn't even up yet, but he could tell by the pale gray of the room that dawn was on its way. His mind traced back over everything from the past couple of days—the revelation from Brandy, his short conversation with Bronson, his time spent with Lori, the kitten . . .

He reached for his phone, and sure enough, there was a text from Lori. She'd sent a list of pet items about twenty minutes ago. Seemed like she hadn't slept much.

*Did you sleep?* he texted back.

*Some,* she replied. *Tiger got the zoomies around 3:00 a.m. and I've been awake since.*

He could only guess what that meant. *If you need a cat-sitter for a couple of hours, I can come grab him. It's still early enough for you to go back asleep.* His phone confirmed it was close to six a.m.

*Thanks for the offer, but I'm already in the shop, getting things ready.*

Malcom stared at her words. Maybe he could take the morning off? He switched over to his calendar to check on the supply delivery schedule. There would be three deliveries this morning alone. He had to oversee them.

*I could grab you breakfast when I'm getting the cat supplies. Let me know what sounds good.*

*Anything sounds good.*

He smiled at that, then wrote, *See you soon.* Or whenever the grocery store opened. A quick Google search told him the grocery store opened at six a.m., so that was good news. He climbed out of bed and took a quick shower. He'd run another day. Right now, Lori needed him.

As he drove out of the parking lot in his truck, he wondered how he'd become so invested in the woman across the street. They were friends—new friends—yet he hadn't ever delivered breakfast to a woman at the crack of dawn. Or bought cat food and cat litter.

Once he reached the grocery store, he stood for several long moments in the pet food aisle. Who knew there were so many choices of cat food and cat litter? How picky was Lori? He texted her photos of the options, hoping she'd be able to reply soon. A couple of minutes later, she told him what to buy, then he loaded everything into the cart and stopped at the deli. He'd bought breakfast here a few times.

He grabbed a couple of burritos that were filled with scrambled eggs, veggies, and bacon, then he picked up a small orange juice too. He didn't know exactly what she liked, but she'd eaten what he'd brought out on a plate at that barbecue, so she didn't seem too picky.

When he parked in front of her shop, the sun was up, and

the clouds looked light and innocent in the sky. Maybe the rain would hold off for the day.

He knocked on the shop's door, not sure if it was open. Moments later, Lori appeared. She opened the door and smiled at him. "You're here."

Malcom smiled back. Lori wasn't wearing any Halloween earrings—too early still? She wore a black sweatshirt with orange lettering that said *Boo!* and black leggings. Her dark hair was braided and hanging over one shoulder.

"I'm here. Hungry?"

"Starving," she said, motioning for him to come inside.

He handed her the sack instead. "I'll grab the cat stuff from my truck. Do you want it upstairs?"

"Sure," she said without hesitation.

He hurried to the truck and hefted the bags, then followed her through the store and up a set of stairs.

"I don't think he's litter trained," Lori said as she opened the door. "He used the newspaper only once, and the rest of the time, he found a different place."

"Is it hard to litter train?" Malcom asked.

"Not usually."

He stepped into an apartment that he could have guessed was hers even if he hadn't been told. He tried not to stare, but that was nearly impossible.

On the opposite wall, three bookshelves stood side by side, crammed with books and decorative items. A small couch—more of a love seat—was draped with an orange-and-black afghan. The other half of the room was a kitchen, and a decorative witch's hat posed as the table's centerpiece.

Beyond the front room, a hallway likely led to the bedroom.

"You can put everything on the table," Lori said.

As he did so, she called out, "Tiger. Malcom's here."

And just like that, as if the kitten had already been trained, it came trotting down the hall.

Malcom crouched and snapped his fingers a couple times. The kitten walked right up to him.

"He remembers you," Lori said, sounding impressed.

While Malcom pet the creature, she dug through the stuff he'd bought. In moments, she had the litter box set up. She scooped up Tiger and set him in the center of the sand. "This is where you go potty," she told him.

The kitten batted around the sand for a moment, then hopped out, shaking off its paws.

"Round one lost?" Malcom asked.

Lori smiled. "I'll win in the end." She washed off her hands, then turned to the sack of food. "Oh, these look good. Stay and eat with me if you want."

"I don't think I have a choice," Malcom said. "Tiger isn't letting me go." The kitten was hanging on to his pant leg and biting at the seam. He tried to pick the cat off, but only got a nip in return. "Ow. Your teeth are sharp."

Lori laughed. "They're just baby teeth, and those are love bites." She pulled out a chair. "Here, sit."

He moved to the table, the kitten still attached to his pant leg. After he sat down, Tiger climbed the rest of the way until he was nestled in Malcom's lap. He looked down at the thing. "He's asleep already? It's like switching off a light."

"Yeah." Lori handed him one of the burritos with a couple of napkins that had been inside the sack. "Cats sleep a lot. Especially kittens."

"Do you really think it was abandoned?"

Lori shrugged. "Only time will tell. I posted a photo on a lost-pets website this morning."

"They have those?" Malcom asked. "Makes sense."

They both started eating, and finally Lori said, "I'd

apologize for the messy state of my apartment, but it's actually the normal state."

He looked about. There were definitely things in every corner and nook and cranny, but he wouldn't call it messy exactly. "It's cozy."

A smile lifted her lips. "That's one way to look at it."

He chuckled. "Really. My mom is a collector of several things. Calendars, old books, all kinds of things."

"What kinds of books?" she asked, her eyes lighting up.

"I don't know exactly—sorry," he said. "I can ask her next time we talk."

"Oh, you don't need to do that, unless you really want to." Lori took a sip of her juice. "I'm just curious if maybe she's collecting classics, or poetry, or just a favorite author."

Malcom blinked. "I never thought to ask, and I haven't checked them out." His gaze strayed to the bookshelves in the other room with their mixture of books and other items. "Do you collect any of those?"

"Not specifically," she said. "I love a used book that's inscribed to someone. You know, like a 'happy birthday' or 'get well' message. It feels like a little memory that lasts forever. Even though they aren't signed to me, it feels like I'm sharing in that memory."

"Huh, I never thought of it that way," Malcom said. "I assumed those books would be hard to sell when someone passes on." The more he got to know Lori, the more interesting she became.

"Not to me." She'd finished the breakfast burrito, and stood to clean things up.

"I can help," he said.

"You have a cat on your lap," she countered.

He chuckled. "True." He couldn't remember a time when he'd felt so relaxed. Or was it peaceful? The morning sun warmed the small kitchen, and he sat in a cozy space, his stomach satisfied, and a purring kitten on his lap. Its fur gleamed gold in the morning light. "Did you give the cat a bath?"

"Yes," Lori said with a huff. "He did not like it, but he smells so good now."

Malcom wasn't about to smell the cat, but he was appreciating the soft, clean fur.

His phone rang, jolting him out of the peaceful morning. Pulling it out of his pocket, he checked the caller. "Sorry, I need to head out."

Lori waved a hand and smiled. "No problem." She moved around the table and scooped up the kitten. "How much do I owe you for the cat supplies?"

"It's on me," he said.

She tilted her head, her eyes soft. "Thanks for everything."

He nodded, wishing he could stay a little longer. If only he didn't have to deal with his brother tonight, he could come back and help her with the event. Or just take care of the kitten.

The rest of the morning and into the afternoon, Malcom was plenty busy. Every time he looked across the street at the shop, he'd see people coming and going. A few booths had been set up on the sidewalk, and once he thought he saw Lori. But it was too hard to tell.

By the late afternoon, Malcom felt jittery, and by the time he headed to his brother's house, he wondered if he was overreacting. Maybe there was a perfectly good explanation for all of this.

On his drive, Penny called. Twice. Malcom let both calls go to voicemail, but instead of leaving a message, she texted him. He glanced at his phone to see that she was trying to meet up with him tonight. Something about a Halloween party. He didn't bother to open the texts.

When he arrived at Bronson's, his brother was just getting out of his car. Talk about perfect timing.

Malcom parked and helped him unload his golf clubs. "How was the tournament?" he asked, even though he didn't want to engage in small talk.

"Came in seventh," Bronson said. "Bunch of cheaters."

Malcom didn't know if his brother was being serious, or if he was just mad about not winning. "I guess it's all for charity in the end, right?"

Bronson shrugged. "Penny's group did well in the women's bracket. They got second place."

"Bronson, you're back?" Kari's voice called out when they walked in through the connecting door from the garage. "We've got a problem."

"Malcom's here," Bronson said just as she appeared.

Her eyes widened for a moment, then she smiled. "Oh nice. What brings you over?"

Malcom hid a frown. "Just need to go over some business stuff with Bronson."

His brother chuckled. "Couldn't wait until tomorrow, I guess. Huh, bro?"

"No, it can't," Malcom answered, trying to keep the edge out of his voice. Was Kari involved in any of this or would she be just as shocked?

"I'd really like a shower first," Bronson said, "but it's probably been a long day for you too?"

"Yeah," Malcom said. "You can shower if you want first. I'm not going anywhere."

In fact, it was probably better. He needed a focused Bronson. Who knew where their conversation would go.

Thirty minutes later, they sat in his home office, which consisted of top-of-the-line computer equipment and deep leather chairs. Kari had brought them drinks and said she'd ordered some dinner for everyone.

Malcom didn't think dinner with him would be happening—at least not on friendly terms.

"What's up?" Bronson asked, leaning back in his office chair, one tanned ankle propped on his knee.

"Let's pull up the accounts receivable spreadsheets on the computer."

Bronson's brow furrowed as he did so.

Malcom spent the next fifteen minutes walking him through everything he had discovered.

Bronson's jaw was tight, but he didn't say much.

"Well?" Malcom asked. "What's going on? Where's the money going?"

"I don't know—it's nothing I did," he said, but his voice was strange-sounding.

"You're the only one besides me with full access to the accounts. Unless Kari knows your passwords? Or Penny?"

It was a low blow to make the accusations, but Malcom needed answers, and Bronson's reaction shouldn't be so passive.

"You're accusing my *wife* of embezzling?" he asked, his voice rising.

"I'm not accusing anyone of anything," Malcom shot back. "I'm asking questions. And if you don't have the answers, then we need to open an investigation."

Bronson's face reddened. "You're just trying to get more money out of this."

"Out of what?" Malcom asked, confused.

"Penny told me you're talking about leaving the company."

Malcom frowned. He'd never said that to Penny. So how could she know anything? He rubbed at his forehead. He hadn't said a thing to anyone—except for Lori. He'd emailed a few contacts over the past couple of months asking for some recommendations. The only way Penny could know any of that would be if she hacked into his email . . . which she could possibly do with his company account.

He stifled a groan. If Penny was hacking into his email, what else was she doing? Gripping his fingers together, he said, "I've been exploring the idea because eventually working twelve-hour days is going to take its toll on me. I don't even remember the last time I took a vacation. Or even a full day off."

Bronson's forehead creased. "If this is about your work hours, we can hire someone to help you with the load."

Malcom jabbed a finger at the spreadsheets. "It's about taxes being misreported and money missing. And now I find out that Penny has been sharing information from my emails—so I don't know what's going on here. But I guess it's time to tell you that I'm leaving the company. I'll stay on as a freelance construction manager for the condo project because I want that job done well, and efficiently. Otherwise, I'll have my lawyer draw up the contract cancellation, and you can figure out the rest of the stuff. Because I'm not going to be liable for what's going on behind my back in the company."

Malcom didn't know he'd made all of these decisions until they came out of his mouth. He pushed to his feet and opened the office door.

Bronson shot to his feet as well. "You're being ridiculous. You can't just make accusations like this, then walk out on me. We built this company together."

Malcom was already halfway down the hallway, heading toward the front door, when he heard, "Bronson, what's going on?" from Kari.

As he opened the door, he heard Bronson tell her in a hushed voice, "Don't say anything more until he's gone. He already knows too much."

Malcom's ears burned, but he continued outside and hurried to his truck. He had some phone calls to make.

# Thirteen

THE WEATHER HELD OFF, JUST barely, which was fine with Lori. As long as it wasn't raining, they could keep all of the booths and activities outside. She'd chosen her black-and-purple wig and added a silk scarf to her ensemble. Some years, she painted her face, but this year, she only wore heavy eye makeup. She had painted her nails black and added several spooky rings, along with necklaces and a pair of bat earrings.

The kids lined up at her table, where she read their palms and gave them wacky predictions, earning a smile and a laugh from them. Everyone seemed to be having a good time, and parents milled on the outskirts as their kids enjoyed themselves. The other carnival booths were also busy, and Lori hadn't realized how late it was until Marci started to pack away the leftover prizes.

"It's already nine o'clock?" she asked. Since it was a school night, they were shutting down earlier than the previous years.

"Yeah, can you believe it?" Marci said. "It's hard to believe Halloween is basically over."

The other vendors who'd brought booths started to clean up. By the time everyone had packed and hauled their stuff away, Lori was feeling how tired she really was. All she wanted was something warm to drink and her kitten.

"I'll see you tomorrow," Marci said, stifling her own yawn. She'd dressed as a scarecrow and had been dropping bits of hay all night. They'd have to sweep in the light of the morning tomorrow.

"Thanks for everything." Lori was turning to head inside, carrying the final box, when she saw someone crossing the street toward the shop. She paused. "Malcom?"

He lifted a hand in greeting. "Hey, sorry I missed the party. How did it all go?"

Lori met his gaze. The man looked tired, yet here he was, asking after her event. "It was really fun. We had a great turnout, and the kids all seemed happy."

"Great news. Can I carry that in for you?"

"I've got it. Besides, looks like you're already carrying something."

He held up a sack she had just noticed. "I brought you some soup in case you're hungry," he said. "Or you can warm it up for another time."

"Oh, thank you."

He grabbed the door handle and pulled it open, and she slipped past him.

"Love your costume," he said. "I thought it would be more witchy though."

She set the box on a nearby table. She'd organize more tomorrow, but right now, she was dead on her feet. The door shut behind Malcom, leaving the two of them in the cozy yellow light of the dimmed shop.

"I'm a fortune teller," she said, spreading her arms, "which doesn't have to be all that witchy."

He chuckled. "The bat earrings are a nice touch, and the purple hair."

Lori grinned as she touched her wig. Then she reached for the sack—it was still warm. "I think I'll eat the soup now before I collapse. What about you? Do you want to share the food?"

He shoved his hands in his pockets. "I already ate, but enjoy."

She tilted her head. "How did it go with your brother?"

His gaze dropped, and after a pause, he said, "Not well. I confronted him, and he denied everything. But I found out Penny's been hacking into my emails, and that Kari is also involved. I've made several phone calls already, hired a lawyer, and I forwarded all of my company emails to a private account since I'm sure my company one will be disabled. Might have already happened by now. I doubt Bronson wasted any time before calling Penny."

"Oh, I'm sorry, Malcom." Lori stepped closer to him, wishing she could erase the pain in his eyes. What must it feel like to be so thoroughly betrayed by a sibling—even if he was a stepbrother. "What can I do to help you?"

Malcom hooked a hand around the back of his neck and blew out a breath. "I don't know what anyone can do—unless you're a lawyer." He gave her a half smile. "I'm leaving the company immediately. I told my brother I'd finish overseeing the condo project, but that's only because I don't want to let Everly Falls down. Although now I'm doubtful of that—I'd have to bill him as a freelance contractor, and that would keep me involved in his financial web."

Lori nodded. She had a lot more questions, but Malcom looked beat. "Come say hi to Tiger at least. He'll make you feel better."

Malcom raised his brows, but he didn't beg off, and in a few seconds, he was following her up the stairs to her apartment.

As soon as she opened the door, Tiger came trotting toward her, meowing.

Lori set the sack on the kitchen table, then scooped up the kitten and crooned, "Are you hungry, little guy?"

Malcom chuckled and pulled out the soup container, and another smaller sack with rolls. Next he drew out a plastic utensil set. "That cat has you wrapped around its little fingers—or claws."

"Haven't you heard?" Lori said. "I'm merely the butler for Tiger—here to fulfill his every command." She put out more cat food, and Tiger settled down to eat, purring. Adorable.

She joined Malcom at the table, where he looked like he was about to wilt. "Are you sure you don't want any?"

"I'm sure," he said.

As she ate, she told him about the costumes she'd seen that night and how cute the kids all were. "I don't mind the older kids coming as well. Marci thinks that trick-or-treaters should be under twelve. But I'm okay with any age."

Malcom frowned. "I hope no one knocked on my trailer door tonight—I mean, I forgot about the candy anyway."

Lori gasped. "You forgot to buy candy for trick-or-treaters? That's like sacrilege."

This earned a genuine laugh from Malcom. "Next year, I'll be sure to make up for it. I'll even decorate." He hesitated. "Although I might be in another trailer somewhere, or maybe living out of my truck."

Lori winced. "You really don't have your own place?"

"I don't," Malcom confirmed. "I need to change that though—eventually. The trailer belongs to the company, so that might not last too long."

"Maybe you can move into your own condominium complex when it's finished?" It was surprising when just as she said it, she was suddenly filled with hope that he'd stick around and live in Everly Falls.

He smiled. "Maybe."

Lori's phone rang, and while it wasn't exactly late at night, it was Halloween. So it was kind of strange. She pulled the phone from her pocket. "Sorry, it's my mom."

Malcom lifted a hand. "Go ahead."

"Hi, Mom," Lori answered, moving to her feet. "What's up?"

"Happy Halloween!"

She exhaled in relief. This was a chatty call, not a "your dad is sick" or "I'm in a crisis" call. "Happy Halloween. Did you have a lot of trick-or-treaters?"

"Not as many as last year, but still a fair number," her mom said. "How did your night go? Did it rain like you'd worried about?"

"No rain," Lori said. "The event went well—kids loved it."

Tiger jumped up on the chair, then the table, meowing. He must have decided the soup smelled better than the cat food. "Tiger, get down," she whispered.

Malcom moved to pick up the cat. Instead of setting him on the ground, he held the kitten to his chest and scratched its ears.

"You're going to spoil him," Lori told him.

"Lori? Who are you with?"

Oh . . . too late to take back the fact that she just revealed she wasn't alone in her apartment.

"Well . . ." she hedged. Malcom had walked over to the couch with the cat still in his arms. Lori moved toward the hallway, not really wanting to share too much with her mom because she'd make a huge deal out of nothing. "I got another cat—a kitten."

"A kitten? Since when?"

"Uh, yesterday. He showed up at my friend's place, all wet and muddy and starving."

"Oh, poor thing," her mom said. "Where were you? Brandy's? How did a kitten get to a place like her cabin?"

"No . . ." Lori sighed and stepped into her bedroom. Malcom could still overhear if he really wanted to. She had to find a way to get out of this conversation, and fast. "I was at my friend Malcom's place for just a few minutes, and we heard the kitten meowing outside. So I brought it home, and he's a busybody but adorable."

"I'm so glad you're okay with getting another cat now," her mom said. "I know how much you miss Silver."

"Yeah, I mean, I didn't have much of a choice. Tiger sort of found me."

"That's a cute name. But tell me about your friend Malcom. Did he go to high school with you?"

Her mom wasn't fooling anyone—she was totally digging for information. "No, he's here on a construction job, working on the condominium complex going up across the street from my shop."

"Lydia Kane told me about that. It sounds terrible."

"It's not terrible—it's needed to sustain the growth in our town," Lori countered. "You had to move away to find a great retirement community, and the kids going off to college aren't coming back."

Her mom went silent at that. But not for long. "So . . . this Malcom. Is he a nice man? Nice enough to date?"

"Yes, but we're friends, that's all. Look, Mom, I really need to go. We'll talk later."

Her mom's voice came through like she was grinning. "I can't wait, honey. Call me first thing tomorrow."

Lori hung up, feeling like she wanted to laugh and groan at the same time. Why did she have to bring up Malcom? There was no way her mom was going to let any of this slide. In fact, her mother now knew things her best friends didn't know. Lori wouldn't put it past her to say something to Lydia and other friends she still had around Everly Falls.

She pulled up the chat group really quick and fired off a short text. *Letting you know I have a new kitten named Tiger. I was hanging out with Malcom last night and we found him. Now you're caught up in case my mom calls one of your moms.*

Julie immediately replied with a laughing emoji. Brandy texted back, *What? You're hanging out with Malcom? Tell us more.*

Lori put her phone on silent. She'd answer in more detail after Malcom left. She'd wanted to call Brandy about the stuff going on with his business, but Lori had been swamped. Besides, she'd leave it to Malcom to share any updates with Brandy.

Sure enough, a solo text arrived from Brandy: *Did Malcom talk to you about our meeting?*

*Yeah,* Lori replied. *It's terrible what his brother has done.* She left it at that and set her phone on the bedside table, then went to find Malcom and Tiger.

But when she walked into the living room, she found him sound asleep on her couch, with Tiger curled next to him. She stood there for a long moment, debating what to do. Wake him and send him on his way? Let him sleep? Maybe the cat would wake him soon anyway? But what should *she* do? Go to bed?

She glanced at the kitchen to see that he'd cleaned everything up. It was kind of hard to stay just friends with this man. He looked absolutely charming asleep on *her* couch. And the addition of the sleeping cat didn't hurt the image at all.

Finally, she decided to turn off the lights save for the one over the stove. She draped a light blanket over Malcom, and Tiger stayed asleep. Then she headed to her room. After leaving her door ajar in case the cat decided to come into her bedroom, Lori changed into her PJs and climbed into bed. She closed her eyes, willing sleep to come, but it wasn't until it started raining softly outside that she finally drifted off.

# Fourteen

FOR THE SECOND MORNING IN a row, Malcom remembered his dreams. This dream, though, wasn't about his brother. Malcom was lying on a giant pillow with a soft, furry blanket that rumbled. Furry? He didn't have furry blankets.

His eyes opened and he found himself staring at a room full of sunshine, bookshelves, and knickknacks. Not his bedroom—definitely not his place.

For a moment, Malcom wondered how he ended up asleep on Lori's couch. They'd been at the kitchen table, then her mom called and . . . what then? He'd put away the soup container and waited on the couch since he didn't want to be rude and leave when she was on the phone.

Next thing he knew, he was waking up.

His pulse spiked, and he patted his pocket for his phone, disturbing a sleeping kitten on his chest. Tiger stretched, kneading his tiny claws into Malcom's chest.

"What are you doing sleeping here? And where's Lori? And how did I sleep so long?" he said to the empty apartment. At least it felt empty.

The kitten nudged his head against Malcom's chin. "All right, I'm getting up. Did you eat breakfast?"

He'd had an amazing night's sleep, and now, he was talking to a cat. He moved to a sitting position, and the kitten leapt off his lap. He looked about for his phone. It was only a hand's reach away on the coffee table. He knew he should check it right away, but he wanted to enjoy the peace for just a moment more.

"Lori?" he called out, just to be sure. No one answered.

He folded the blanket that had been draped over him—by Lori—and stood. A peek down the hallway showed him that the bed in her room was made, and all was quiet. He spied a handwritten note on the kitchen table.

Picking it up, he read: *I'm in the shop. Help yourself to whatever you can find in the kitchen.* Malcom did feel hungry, but maybe it was because the morning was half over. A glance at the microwave clock told him it was nearly ten. Thankfully, he knew there weren't any deliveries until this afternoon. But even from this distance, he could hear the rumble of construction trucks through the window.

He had to get a move on and deal with the fallout from his brother.

Maybe he wasn't hungry after all.

He turned from the window, only to have his foot attacked by a frisky kitten. Tiger seemed to have forgotten that Malcom was a hundred times his size.

"What are you doing, crazy cat?" he said, scooping up the wriggling ball of fur that couldn't decide if it wanted to purr or bite his fingers. "It appears you're going to have a better day than me."

He decided it wasn't strange to be talking to a cat. That's what pet owners did, right? Not that he was a pet owner. He set down the kitten, then picked up his phone without looking at the screen. He'd get back to his trailer, shower, and dress for the day before he read any messages or emails.

Before leaving the apartment, he paused and looked around. The place was all Lori, and it really was cozy. Maybe he should start looking for an apartment—in Everly Falls? It had been a long time since he'd slept so deeply and felt so . . . content. Was it being in a place that wasn't a trailer? Was it Lori? Was it Everly Falls?

He didn't know.

Malcom left the apartment, shutting the kitten on the other side of the door. As he headed down the stairs, he wondered what Tiger would be doing all day while Lori worked. He paused at the bottom of the stairs. Turning left would take him directly outside. Turning right would take him into the shop.

He turned right. Lori was with a customer. Someone he recognized.

"Malcom?" Brandy said, her brows shooting straight up. Her hair was scooped into a high ponytail, and she wore athletic clothing, which only reminded him that he'd missed both running and the gym the past several days.

Brandy's gaze cut to Lori, where she stood by the large front window that she was transforming from Halloween stuff to what looked like Thanksgiving decorations.

"Surprise," Lori told her. "But it's not what you think."

Brandy folded her arms, her eyebrows cocked. "That's what they all say."

"I fell asleep on Lori's couch," Malcom said, noting the pink that had stolen into her cheeks. She had dressed in jeans this morning—blue—which surprised him. Her shirt was even more surprising, or maybe it wasn't. She wore a long-sleeved yellow T-shirt with a printed *Gobble Gobble* on the front. Her hair was in its usual ponytail, and her earrings . . . gold turkeys.

It was impossible to hide his smile. So the all-black clothing wasn't a year-round thing? Just an October thing?

"Thanks, by the way," he said, looking only at Lori. "For letting me sleep. I guess I zonked out."

"You did." Lori's blush deepened, but her blue eyes sparkled. "Tiger wasn't going to let you go anywhere."

Malcom chuckled. "He *was* insistent."

Brandy's gaze flitted back and forth between the two of them.

"Did you eat?" Lori asked, sounding slightly breathless. "Brandy brought in some bagels."

"I'll eat later," he said. "But thanks."

"Well, well, well," Brandy said with a smirk. "I guess that's all settled. Malcom, how is everything going with your brother? Lori said I had to ask you."

His gut tightened. "I haven't checked my phone yet, but I told my brother I'm leaving the company. I did retain a lawyer last night to handle the transition."

"Oh wow." Brandy's expression filled with compassion. "Did your brother explain what happened?"

"No, he denied everything, but there was enough there that I know he's covering up." Malcom raked a hand through his hair. "I've been wanting to step away for a while now, anyway, I just didn't think I'd be doing it on these terms."

"I'm really sorry," Brandy said. "If you need to talk to anyone, I know Ian would be a good sounding board."

"Thanks," Malcom said. "I'll reach out to him later."

Lori picked up a sack from a nearby table. "Here, take this. Something to eat at least. And if there's anything I can help with, let me know."

Her words weren't platitudes—that, Malcom knew. The sincerity in her gaze was proof enough. "I don't want to take your breakfast," he said.

The edge of Lori's mouth lifted, and she practically shoved the sack into his hands. "It's fine. I can grab something from upstairs anyway. Today will be a slow day here—Halloween hangover."

Malcom nodded. "All right, then." He paused. "Thanks again. For everything. And sorry I fell asleep on you—I mean, on your couch."

Brandy laughed, and Lori's cheeks were back to pink.

By the time he reached his trailer, his stomach was grumbling. So it was that he ate breakfast first, then showered, then checked his phone.

It was like his phone had been lit with fireworks. His brother had called several times and left voicemails. Penny had texted and called. His new lawyer had called. His dad had called. And his mom had called.

What in the world?

Malcom called his mom first.

"Oh, there you are," she said, relief in her voice. Her marriage with her second husband had only lasted a few years, but now she was remarried again, living in Montana. Phil was a nice guy, by all that Malcom could see.

"How are you?" he asked, thinking that maybe this phone call had nothing to do with the construction company problems.

"I'm not calling for small talk, Malcom," she said in a brisk tone. "What's going on between you and your brother? I had to hear everything from your father. You know I don't like to know things second or third hand."

"I know that," Malcom said, his mind racing. What had Bronson told their father? "What did Dad say?" It was the safest question since he wasn't ready to tell her of his suspicions and accusations. Especially if things continued going south and charges had to be filed.

"That you're ditching the company and leaving Bronson high and dry." His mom's voice turned shrill. "Why would you do that to your stepbrother? You're the glue of that place, and you know it. Without you, everything will crumble."

Malcom wasn't exactly surprised at the misinformation his mom had been given. Very one-sided, it seemed. Yet he didn't want to state his case because, again, what if he said something that was used against him later on? He wasn't thinking his mom had any ill intentions toward him, but their relationship was complicated. She'd basically chosen a man, who wasn't his father, over him—and moved out of the country. Started a completely separate life from her teenaged son.

He didn't begrudge her finding happiness in a relationship with another man, but it had taken Malcom a long time to shake the feelings of being abandoned. Or discarded like it wasn't a big deal to have his entire life uprooted.

"Mom, sorry you had to find out this way," he said. "I've been wanting a change for a while. Bronson can hire another manager."

"But you're brothers," she said. "You've been best friends. Your dad is devastated. Bronson is devastated."

Now her words were getting under his skin. "Have you talked to Bronson too?"

That made her pause. "Well, no, but your dad told me all about it. I don't need to talk to Bronson to know how much you've hurt him."

Malcom swallowed down a scoff. "Like I said, sorry I didn't talk to you before you heard from Dad. But things are already in motion, and believe me, I'll be better off in the long run."

"What about Bronson? What about your father?"

Malcom pinched the top of his nose and closed his eyes. His father had invested in their company in the beginning, giving them some seed money so they'd qualify for the bank loan in the first place. "Dad has earned back his investment already. He'll be fine—if that's what you're asking."

"It's not money I'm talking about," his mom said. "This is family—the most important thing we have on Earth."

What was this? A spiritual talk? If anything, his mom had created—and divorced—too much family.

He exhaled. "Look, Mom, I should really go. I need to call Dad too."

"Oh, he's right here."

Nothing could have surprised Malcom more. "What do you mean? Are you not back in California?"

"No, your father is with me in Montana."

That didn't sound right . . . what was going on?

"What do you mean, *with* you?"

She laughed. "Well, it turns out, there's still something between us."

"What about Phil?" Malcom asked. "You know, your husband?"

"Oh, we're separated, honey. I didn't want to bother you with the drama since you've been so swamped with the new condo project."

Malcom's mind reeled. His *parents* were back together? After how many years? "Mom, I'm never too busy to talk to you. This is news I should have known . . . What about Dad's wife?"

Another laugh. "They're getting a divorce."

"Since *when*?"

"Oh, a few weeks, maybe."

"I don't understand . . ." he said, a headache now appearing with full force. "You and Dad divorced and totally upended our lives, and now you're back together and laughing about each other's divorces?"

"Life's strange, isn't it," his mom said.

Malcom had no words anymore.

"But really, Malcom, what were you thinking? You need to call Bronson right now and apologize."

He blew out a breath. This was what he was getting out of his mom—another upside-down revelation of how she and his dad were back together? But her real concern was that he needed to play nice with a stepbrother who was likely a criminal?

"Look, I need to go," he said. "I have to wade through a lot of things."

"Oh, I know, you're always busy," his mom said in a flippant tone. "Call your brother before you do anything else."

Then she hung up.

Malcom couldn't quite believe it. Was he in a living dream—or more accurately, a nightmare?

He crossed to the door of the trailer and opened it. Standing in the doorway for several minutes, he breathed in the crisp autumn air. Everything seemed to be going smoothly on the construction site right now. His gaze strayed toward Lori's shop. He couldn't make out the exact details of her window decorations, but it looked like she'd made a lot of progress already.

He kind of wished he were still asleep on her couch. He couldn't explain it, but he felt comfortable around her. And that dang kitten was pretty cool too. But mostly, Lori was easy to talk to, easy to be with, easy to be himself around, and of course, not hard on the eyes.

Okay, so she was beautiful, and he loved how it was all natural. Not primped and preened like Penny. He thought back to the moments before he'd zonked out the night before when she'd gotten that phone call from her mom. Hearing part of the one-sided conversation, he could tell her mom was asking about him—and Lori was trying to brush it off quickly. Which was fine. They were just friends, after all.

His phone rang, jolting him out of his straying thoughts. Penny was calling.

There was no way he was taking her call. And yes, he'd checked to see that his company email account had been disabled—which he'd have to inform his lawyer about. Besides, he'd rather talk to his brother instead of Penny, which was saying a lot. He sent the call to voicemail.

Then he called his lawyer.

# Fifteen

LORI'S GROUP CHAT WITH HER friends had been lighting up all evening with chatter about their planned dinner the next night. Everyone, including significant others, would be meeting at Everly and Austin's place. Lori was determined to go since she still felt a little guilty about leaving the weekend getaway early.

She set her hands on her hips and surveyed the light bulb strip above the bathroom mirror in her parents' old house. The once-silver base was faded and chipped. It would have to be replaced. How hard could it be to replace a light fixture? She'd simply go to the hardware store, buy a light fixture and follow the instructions.

*Does 6:30 work for everyone?* Everly wrote in her text. *I have to take Jessica to a friend's birthday party at 6:00 p.m.*

*Sure, that works for us,* Julie wrote.

Everyone else put a check mark on Everly's text.

Lori pocketed her phone. She'd tackle this project tomorrow, or the next day. She needed to do a final check on the shop, something she always did, even when Marci closed. She turned off the lights, left the house, and headed back to her place.

As she pulled around the shop to park, she noted with

pride how great the window display looked with the Thanksgiving decor in place. Marci had put in a couple of extra hours to help, which Lori was grateful for. She climbed out of her car and headed through the back door of the shop.

A quick check told her everything was in order, and she went upstairs to her apartment.

Tiger greeted her at the door, and she scooped up the furry bundle. "I missed you," she crooned to the kitten.

Tiger licked her chin, then began to purr. Oh, how she'd missed having a pet.

"Malcom is missing out," she told him. "I wonder what he's up to."

She hadn't heard from Malcom all day. She'd even taken over some cookies from the local bakery, but he hadn't answered when she'd knocked on the door of his trailer. His truck had been parked nearby, so maybe he was on a phone call or something. Or even napping. Whatever was going on, she didn't want to pester him with a text or phone call.

Lori stroked her fingers over Tiger's furry back as she walked into the kitchen to get a drink. The kitten purred away, sounding like a rumbling motorcycle.

The group chat was now in the throes of deciding the food for tomorrow night's dinner.

*What can I bring?* Lori wrote. She'd have to find time to grocery shop tomorrow since she was pretty much out of everything. Which was kind of ironic, considering the note she'd left Malcom that morning to help himself to anything in the kitchen. She wondered if he'd looked around and found nothing.

*Potluck 100% or assigned potluck?* Brandy wrote.

*Let's get crazy,* Everly wrote. *Potluck 100%.*

*Not even assigning main dishes or desserts?* Stephenie asked.

*Come at your own risk,* Everly texted. *Or should I say, eat at your own risk.*

A series of laughing emojis from all the women filled Lori's phone screen. She'd definitely bring a main dish. It would be funny if everyone brought a dessert, but not very satisfying.

*Are you bringing Malcom?* Brandy texted.

Lori groaned. Leave it to Brandy to bring him up—and in front of the whole group. Now there would be a bunch of questions.

*You're worse than my mom,* Lori texted. *And that's saying something.*

*"Friends" are welcome,* Brandy wrote, then added a winking emoji.

Lori didn't commit to anything. She just added a *haha* to Brandy's text.

She blew out a breath. She *could* ask him—it wouldn't hurt to do that. But did she want more scrutiny from her friends? And did he want to be in a social situation while he was dealing with whatever was going on with the company and his brother? What *was* going on? Had there been progress? New revelations? Bad news? Good news?

Lori moved to the kitchen window that overlooked the street. The sun was in its final stages of setting, and in the purple twilight, she could see that a light was on in the trailer across the street. Malcom's truck was parked next to it. She'd noticed it had been gone the last couple of hours. But now, apparently, he'd returned.

Maybe she could text him. Just something friendly and casual to check in. She wouldn't make him feel obligated to respond. Even though she told herself that, she still wanted him to. Was it selfish to want to ease her own worry? Inviting him to dinner the next night could be an ice breaker.

"What do you think, Tiger?" Lori said. "Should we go visit our friend Malcom?"

Tiger purred in response.

Lori didn't know why she thought that heading to Malcom's with the kitten was a good idea, but that's what she did a few minutes later. She'd bundled up Tiger in a blanket so he wouldn't get scared and leap out of her arms.

Her heart was pounding by the time she reached the trailer, and she second-guessed herself more than once. But she'd made it this far... She knocked on the trailer door, and moments later, it opened.

Malcom stood there, wearing a T-shirt and shorts, hair damp. Had he just taken a shower? He smiled, and it gave her a little more courage.

"Hi," she said. "Tiger wanted to see you."

He chuckled. "Is that so? Bring him inside. It's getting cold."

It was getting cold, although the daylight hours had been mild.

"Good timing," he said. "I just got back from a run and showered."

Tiger wriggled at the sound of Malcom's voice, and once the door was shut, Lori let the kitten out of the confines of the blanket.

Tiger meowed at Malcom, and he picked the kitten up. "Thanks for the cookies by the way," he told Lori. "I haven't had a chance to text you yet."

"Everything going okay?" she asked.

"Define okay," he said, irony in his tone. He settled at the kitchen table, and she sat across from him.

He looked less stressed than he had the night before. "You went for a run, so that's good."

He nodded and scratched the top of Tiger's head—the kitten immediately started purring. "It's remarkable that such a small cat can make so much noise." Malcom paused, then lifted his hazel gaze. "My partnership with my brother has been dissolved—I've already signed everything on my end."

Despite knowing he'd wanted to leave the company, doing it this way was rough. "I'm sorry about all of this—especially your brother's role."

Malcom released the kitten, and it strutted across the table to Lori. "I am too. I do hope that someday I'll get the real story. I don't know where the breakdown happened—was it my brother's idea? Kari's? Penny's? They're all involved. It seems I was the only one in the dark. And I keep asking myself why they'd do this—is money really so important to risk fraud charges and family relationships?"

Lori's heart hurt because even though Malcom's tone was matter-of-fact, she could see the pain in the depths of his eyes. "Have you talked to any of them today, or are you letting your lawyer handle everything?"

"I talked to my brother this morning—well, 'talk' is a relative word," Malcom said. "He brought up a bunch of stuff from our high school days, stuff I thought we'd worked through. He accused me of always trying to take the limelight, stealing his friends, stealing his scholarship opportunities. None of which is true."

"So this was all payback?" she asked.

He rubbed a hand over his face. "It's the only thing that makes sense. I mean, I think it started out as just wanting to keep tabs on me and profiting from my work—but I truly believe that once he married Kari and Penny got involved, things escalated."

"But Penny was trying to date you—how does that all factor in?"

"That's a good question," Malcom deadpanned. "Maybe to have more control over me? To monitor me more?"

Lori winced. "As terrible as it sounds, it kind of makes sense."

He gave her a half smile, a sad smile. "Like I said, someday I'd like the full story, but right now, I just want this to all go away. As if I never knew any of them." He exhaled. "I've had to take myself off the condominium project. My lawyer says that even if I worked as an independent contractor, it would muddy up the legal waters."

Lori stared at him. "You're out of a job?"

He spread his hands. "As of five p.m., I've been unemployed."

Her mind spun. Would Malcom leave Everly Falls, then? "What are your plans?" she asked in a careful voice.

"Good question," he said. "I've set up my LLC. Austin texted me today and wants to meet tomorrow."

This surprised Lori, but maybe she shouldn't be. "As an architect, he probably has a lot of connections. Does that mean you'd be staying in Everly Falls?"

"I've never been opposed to it." His gaze held hers for a couple of seconds.

"I wouldn't be opposed to it either," she said. "I mean, you already have friends. In fact, we're doing a dinner tomorrow night at Everly and Austin's place, and I'm on strict orders to invite you."

"I could go," he said, his gaze leveled with hers again. "Do you want me to go?"

"I'm fine with it," she said with a smirk. "I told everyone that we're strictly friends."

"Right, strictly," he echoed, a bit hollow-sounding. "Do you want a drink or anything?" He stood and moved to the small fridge.

"Water would be great," she said. "I don't want to put you out. I should have brought over some dinner. Are you hungry?"

"Not really." He pulled out a water bottle from the fridge

and handed it to her. "I seem to have lost my appetite after talking to my mom, although I did eat one of those cookies you dropped off."

Lori took a sip of the water. "You talked to your mom too? Is she involved, or was she just concerned?" She winced when she realized how her question sounded.

Malcom leaned against the table, his arms folded. "Well, apparently, she's separated from her current husband, and my dad is getting a divorce from his wife, and now my parents are back together."

Lori stared. "What? I don't get it, I thought you said your mom was finally in a great marriage and . . ." She stopped talking at the sight of the angst on Malcom's face.

"That's what I thought too." He scrubbed a hand through his damp hair. "I'm not sure if I'm more bothered by my parents' news or my brother's betrayal. Heck, I feel betrayed by everyone in my family right now."

"It's a lot," Lori said in a quiet voice. Her heart literally hurt for him, and she could only imagine what he must feel like. "Awful, really." She stood and moved toward Malcom.

He watched her approach, and her heart seemed to tug her closer. She wrapped her arms around him and hugged him. After a couple of seconds, he pulled her close.

Lori tried not to let herself be distracted by his clean shower scent, or the warmth of his torso, or the strength of his arms about her. She should be the one giving *him* strength. The hug continued, morphing from comfort to feeling intimate. Then she felt tiny pricks on her calf and realized Tiger was climbing up her leg.

"Ow." She drew away with a laugh and grasped his wriggly body. "You want attention too?"

Malcom took the kitten. "He's just jealous that you're hugging me."

Lori laughed, her stomach feeling tight with nerves. Had the hug been too much? But then Malcom grasped her hand.

"Thanks for coming over," he said in a soft voice. "I appreciate all you've done."

Lori drew in a thready breath. His fingers were warm, steady, strong. "I've done hardly anything. I'm happy to go grab dinner for you."

"How about we go together and pick up something, then eat at your place? Let Tiger loose?"

And that's how they ended up sitting on her couch, takeout on the coffee table, with some random comedy show on the television, and Tiger sleeping on Malcom's chest. When the show ended, Lori turned it off, thinking that Malcom would go home soon.

But they continued to talk for another hour, until both of them started to yawn.

"Looks like you're spending the night on the couch again," she said.

"It's not like I have to get up early to work," he said in an amused tone. "I have plenty of time to be a cat bed."

Lori laughed. She loved that Malcom's mood seemed lighter. They'd talked more about his parents and his childhood while they ate dinner. She could see the pain that the divorce had caused him, and now the confusion of his parents' relationship. He also let her listen to the voicemails from Penny. His lawyer had told him to save them. The first couple were sickly sweet, then the last one full of threats.

Threats that had no power since Malcom was no longer part of the company.

"My couch is always available," Lori teased. She reached over to pet the kitten lightly. Malcom grasped her hand and threaded their fingers, making her pulse thrum.

"Is this okay?" he asked, his voice a low rumble.

Lori looked at their intertwined hands, his large, callused, strong. "It's okay." It was more than okay, but she didn't want to presume. This man could be heading out of Everly Falls any day.

His thumb stroked her fingers, and goose bumps raced along her arm. "I like hanging out with you," he said. "It's like we've known each other a lot longer than a month."

Her breath caught. "I like hanging out with you too."

"What was your mom asking you about last night—before I fell asleep here?"

"Oh." Lori's cheeks heated at his question, but also because he was still holding her hand. "She wanted to know all about the kitten, of course, and she was very interested in my new friend."

He smirked. "What did you tell her?"

"That we're strictly friends." Although right now, it felt anything but.

"There's that *strictly* word again," he said, the edges of his mouth curving.

She wondered what was going on behind those hazel eyes of his.

"I really should get going, though," he said. "I'm getting way too comfortable here and could fall asleep at any moment."

He did look tired, but his sleepiness was still appealing.

"Let me remove your encumbrance." Gently, she lifted Tiger from his chest. "There, you're free to go."

Tiger stretched, then hopped off the couch and trotted away. "Did I tell you he's litter-trained now?" she said. Talking about the kitten was a much safer subject than their friendship status.

Malcom's brows lifted. "Already? He's growing up so fast. I'm so proud."

She laughed, then pushed to her feet. A little distance from Malcom would be good. He was too close, too easy to hang out with— it was too tempting to cross the friendship line.

"Let me know how your meeting with Austin goes tomorrow," she said. "You're still good for the dinner later?"

"I am." Malcom stood, and Lori found that they were only inches away from each other. The sun had set hours ago, and the room was lit with only one lamp, leaving most of the room in shadow.

"Thanks for inviting me, and for including me in your friend group," he said. "Brandy has been really helpful, and I suspect things will go well with Austin tomorrow too."

Lori folded her arms because goose bumps were racing along them at his nearness. "I hope they will. I mean, it would be really great if you stayed around." She gave a nonchalant shrug. "There are places to rent, like that apartment complex on the other side of town. And of course, there's always my couch and Tiger."

The edges of his mouth lifted. "I'll let you know."

She nodded, and expected him to step away and walk to the door. But he didn't move, and she felt her heart rate double when he continued looking at her, his gaze lowering to her mouth.

Was he . . . ?

When his hand lifted, and his fingers skimmed her jaw, she whispered, "What are you doing?"

"I want to kiss you, Lori."

She drew in a breath, her pulse roaring in her ears. "Do you think that's a good idea?"

"I'd like to find out." His hand slipped to the nape of her neck, and the touch of his fingers on her skin made everything heat inside of her.

She tentatively placed a hand on his chest, even though one part of her was telling her to step back, keep a safe distance from this man. To guard her heart. Yet she could feel his heart racing beneath his shirt, and ignoring any logic, she curled her fingers into the fabric and tugged him toward her.

His smile appeared.

Lifting her chin, she met his mouth. His lips were warm and soft, yet firm. Kissing Malcom wasn't a good idea, her mind said, but her body wasn't listening. Her eyes slid shut, and she let her body respond to his.

Malcom's mouth moved over hers, slow and deliberate, like he wasn't in any hurry. Like this wasn't a rushed or impulsive decision. Like kissing her had been planned and very much on purpose. She wrapped her arms about his neck and seemed to fit perfectly against his torso. She tangled her fingers into his hair, and he responded by angling his mouth and taking their kiss deeper. One of his hands cradled her neck, and the other hand anchored her hips against his.

The kissing heated up, and she knew it could easily combust. Which meant she had to ease back. She moved her hands to his shoulders and put a half inch space between their bodies.

She felt his sigh. Was he regretting it already?

He lifted his head, his eyes dark pools, and his fingers a light touch on her jaw. "Should I apologize?" he asked in a raspy tone.

"Only if you think kissing me was a mistake," she whispered.

"It wasn't a mistake, but I know that you don't want to date anyone." His gaze was warm, teasing, but also hopeful.

The look in his eyes made her entire body flood with her own hope. "Well, maybe I'll change my mind if you decide to stick around."

His other hand left her hip and trailed up her back in a slow caress. "You're giving me a pretty good reason to stay."

She had to kiss him for saying that, so she did.

Malcom smiled against her lips. "Trying to bribe me?"

"Maybe," she murmured.

# Sixteen

MALCOM HAD BEEN SCREENING A lot of calls all morning, but when the phone number for the mayor of Everly Falls, Alice Sanders, popped up, he had to answer.

"Malcom," she said, diving right in. "What's happening with your company's bankruptcy? Please tell me the condominium project isn't going to grind to a halt."

Malcom couldn't react for a moment. *Bankruptcy?* Was that how Bronson was going to try getting out of his mess? He crossed the small office space of the trailer and sank onto the desk chair.

"Are you there, Malcom?" Mayor Sanders's voice came through the phone.

"Yes, I'm here," he said. "Sorry, Mayor, I don't know what to say. I dissolved myself from the partnership yesterday. From everything I was told, the project would continue without me."

"You're the reason we agreed to the project in the first place," the mayor said, her voice growing sharper. "And now . . . I don't know what to say. Only that we're not letting a construction site go fallow while your company is in bankruptcy hearings. This is a lawsuit that's waiting to happen."

Malcom didn't correct her on calling it his company. His mind raced as he tried to think of other solutions. The only one that would solve everything was for another company to buy out Bronson from the project. But any other company probably had a booked-out schedule. "I understand about the lawsuit," he told the mayor. "Look, if it were up to me, my former company would finish the project. I even offered to contract as the construction manager until it's finished, but my lawyer advised against it."

"Isn't your partner your brother?" the mayor asked in a softer tone.

"Yes," Malcom said. "Although it turns out that wasn't in my favor, and there were some . . . things that I couldn't work with, so I withdrew. I didn't want it to affect Everly Falls, but I really had no choice."

"What things?" she asked.

"Personal things that turned into company issues," he said, not willing to go down the path of confiding in her. Only Lori knew the full details. "Look, can I call you at the end of the day? I want to do some due diligence and see if I can come up with a solution."

"I hope you can," the mayor said. "My entire office is up in arms, and it won't take long for the news to reach the rest of the town."

"I understand." Malcom hung up, the ideas forming in his head faster than he could weigh each one. What if . . . ? He rubbed his forehead. It would be a leap. A major commitment. A huge investment.

Drawing in a breath, he picked up his phone again and sent Austin a text: *I'm on my way.*

Fifteen minutes later, he was sitting across from Austin Hayes in a corner booth of the diner. His dark brown eyes studied Malcom as they waited for their order to arrive.

"What's the update?" Austin asked.

Malcom had given him the bare minimum in a previous phone call. "I just found out that Bronson filed for bankruptcy and the condominium project is at an indefinite stall."

Austin visibly winced. "The townspeople will be furious."

"Yeah . . ." Malcom conceded. "Mayor Sanders already called me. She's threatening a lawsuit. I wouldn't be surprised if she sued me in addition to my brother's company."

Austin nodded. "Things could get a lot worse before they get better, which is why I wanted to meet with you. My company, Hayes Architecture, has been hired to renovate the natural history museum in town."

Malcom didn't know the place, but he'd been working nonstop since he'd arrived, and hadn't exactly had time for sightseeing.

"You're probably guessing what I'm going to ask," Austin continued. "I need to hire a good manager."

Malcom might be flattered, but he was also practical. "Don't you already have one?"

"This job's timing would conflict with two other projects in neighboring towns," Austin said. "So I really could use the help. It would give you a buffer while you're building up your own business. With you on board, the project would finish before the deadline, which could get you into the good graces of the mayor again."

Austin said the last bit with a smile, but Malcom didn't return it.

"I'd be a fool to turn it down," he said. "But right now, I need to find a way to keep the condo project from turning into a wasteland for the next year until another company buys the whole thing, or a lawsuit is completed, and the city sends it out for more bids."

The server appeared and set down their platters of food. Both had ordered chicken parmesan meals.

Austin took a sip of his soda. "What are your options?"

At this, Malcom sighed. "I need to do a bunch of the legwork to find someone to take over the project. I have a lot of contacts in the industry. And the sooner I do it, the better. I'd like to be able to give the mayor good news before word gets out to everyone else."

Austin gave a thoughtful nod as he cut a piece of his chicken and ate a bite. "I can put out my feelers too. Too bad my company doesn't do new builds. We only handle renovations."

"I understand, but I was hoping you'd be a good sounding board for starters."

"Oh?"

Malcom pulled out the printed report he'd brought with him and unfolded it. "This is my project projection for the build. It shows all the incoming and outgoing expenses, and payroll, plus the estimated profit."

Austin took the report and leafed through it. When he got to the final page, he let out a low whistle. "That's a good chunk of change."

"It reflects several months of work." Malcom reached over and tapped one of the lines. "This also reflects a decent discount we gave the city because some of the vendors are from Everly Falls, which saves money on transportation and shipping."

"You're using Jennings Carpet Company?" Austin asked. "That's great."

"Yeah." Malcom folded his hands atop the table. "With this project at a stall, all of these deals will be delayed or even canceled. As an example, a new construction company coming in might have their own carpet company they already contract with."

Austin lifted his gaze. "I see what you're saying. This bankruptcy is going to affect a lot of people."

"Yeah." Malcom drew in a breath. "I feel responsible in a way." He explained his suspicions about his brother's fraud and how everything crumbled from there.

"Wow," Austin said. "That's rough no matter how you look at it."

"I'm not in a position to take over the project on my own," Malcom said. "I'd need investors, and the rest secured through a bank loan. But within a year, with only fifty percent of the condos sold, it would turn a profit."

Austin put down his fork. "You're thinking of taking it over?"

"The thought's been nagging me," he admitted. "It might not be attainable though. I haven't run any hard numbers yet, and I haven't talked to any investors, or approached a bank. I'd need a good down payment, of which I can come up with about half. The rest would have to be a construction loan."

Austin flipped through the report again. "I might be interested. Can you send me the report when you have more concrete numbers, and I'll talk through things with my dad? He works with me, and I don't know how he'll feel, but I'm mostly interested in this because it's Everly Falls."

Malcom felt elated at Austin's interest, but there was still a long way to go. He scrubbed a hand through his hair. "I understand. I'll get to work on the numbers." He paused. "I wouldn't be doing this either if this were any other location. I mean, it's kind of like putting my whole life on the line."

Austin chuckled. "You believe in it, and that's a good sign. The best sign. It would certainly make the mayor happy if this project could be salvaged without too much trouble." He took another sip of his drink. "Are you going to stay in the trailer, or are you going to find a more permanent place to stay?"

"I need to be out of the trailer soon," he said. "It's in the company name, which is no longer mine. I'm not sure how permanent I can commit to until I figure out if I can get a business loan for the project."

"There's a house for rent on our street," Austin said. "Everly pointed it out to me the other day, and said it might be a good place for someone like you."

Malcom raised his brows. "That's a coincidence."

Austin grinned. "I think she's looking out for her friend Lori."

"Lori doesn't factor into this decision." When he saw the disbelief on Austin's face, he continued, "I mean, she's definitely a good part of Everly Falls. But there are many good things about this town. I've enjoyed my time here so far."

Austin's smile appeared again. "I get it. You've only known each other a few weeks. But when you know, you know."

Malcom wanted to get off the subject of Lori—if he confessed anything, he had no doubt it would make it back to Everly, then the entire friend group. He couldn't do that to her. They'd kissed last night, and he was pretty sure she wanted that development to stay between them. "How was it when you met Everly? You're not originally from here."

Austin finished another bite of his food. "I definitely wasn't looking to move out of my own town. My daughter had a good situation and routine with my parents helping out. I hadn't realized what Jessica was missing out on without having a mom around. And me—what I was missing out on. Until we met Everly. Things fell into place after that."

"That's great," Malcom said. "You guys are wonderful together. And you've been great to me. So thank you."

"It's not a problem," Austin said. "You're a good man. And it's plain that Lori sees it too—and all her friends."

Malcom wasn't sure if he'd ever received so many compliments at once.

"I guess we'll see you tonight?" Austin asked.

"I'll be there," he said. "But keep this idea of mine between us for now. I don't want to set up any expectations in case things don't pan out."

Austin nodded and set his napkin on the table. "No problem."

After they parted ways, Malcom walked back to the building site and his trailer. He hadn't driven his truck, preferring to walk. Take in the sights of the town that he was thinking of staying a while in. Maybe. Time would tell. Before the dinner with Lori and her friends, he wanted to reach out to the construction crew—let them know that he was trying to find a way to keep them employed. He'd need their patience though.

Everything seemed to be happening at once, and he wasn't sure he could pull it all off. In the middle of all his swirling thoughts, there was Lori. And their kiss last night. It had been on the edge of all of his decisions today. Austin had probably been right. Lori was definitely part of this decision. At least the decision to find a place other than a trailer to live in.

There'd been no communication between them since saying goodbye last night. What if she regretted things? What if she regretted him? His life was a chaotic mess right now, and she didn't even know about the bankruptcy.

He pulled out his phone to call her, or maybe text her. She deserved an update.

But he'd rather see her and talk to her in person. Would the shop be busy now? There was only one way to find out.

When he reached the shop, he paused at the window display decorated for Thanksgiving. It made him smile to think that Lori was probably wearing a turkey-themed shirt or something with a cornucopia. He wondered what her earrings would be. Then he wondered if she ever wore the same earrings twice.

The bell jangled when he opened the door, and seconds later, he was greeted by Marci.

"Oh, hello, there," she said with a wide smile. Her red hair was held in place by a dark green headband that matched her green sweater. "Looking for Lori?"

Before he could answer, she called out, "Lori, he's here."

*He's here?* Did he not need a name?

"I think I'll take my lunch break now," Marci continued. She flashed Malcom a smile. "She's in the storage room."

Then Marci was gone before Malcom could even get a single word in. He stood for a moment after the woman sailed out of the shop. Then he heard footsteps and turned.

Lori had appeared, a roll of orange ribbon and a pair of scissors in her hands. "Oh, hey."

Her expression was calm, but her eyes were curious, questioning even. She wore russet-brown overalls, a long-sleeved shirt, and yes . . . earrings that looked like miniature autumn leaves.

"Hey," he said.

The air between them seemed to pause. He wasn't sure what the right thing to say was. Was she happy about last night? Regretting it? Were things different in the light of day?

"How did the lunch with Austin go?" she asked.

She didn't make a move to walk any closer, but he didn't like the distance between them.

"It went great, actually." He took a few steps, closing the distance. Her chin lifted, and her eyes remained on his, her gaze steady. He liked that.

"I meant to call you this morning," he said. "There've been some new developments with Bronson."

"What's going on?" she asked, setting the ribbon and scissors on a nearby display shelf.

He gave her a quick rundown, then said, "I'm working on some solutions so the town doesn't get jilted."

A smile touched her face. "Of course you are. I'm not surprised in the least."

He was surprised though—at her confidence in him. "You're not?"

"No." Her voice dipped low. "Are you still planning on dinner tonight with my friends?"

He noted the hope in her eyes, and knew her question wasn't as simple as it sounded. "Do you still want me to go?"

"I do."

He stepped close then and touched one of her earrings. "I like these."

She huffed out a laugh. "You always say that."

His heart felt like it was zooming about the room. "It's always true." He leaned closer, and when she didn't move, he pressed his mouth against hers.

The kiss was light, intermingled with smiling, and filled with plenty of warmth.

Her hands slid up his chest, creating a trail of fire, and he anchored his hands at her waist. He didn't dare pull her too close or take the kiss too deep. The shop was open, and they could be interrupted at any moment. But he definitely enjoyed kissing her, and he couldn't decide if this second round was better than the first. Maybe equal?

He liked having her in his arms. Her skin soft, her touch warm, her scent cinnamon.

"Are we kissing friends now?" she asked, drawing away much too soon.

It took a moment for his mind to comprehend her question because he'd become lost in her touch. "It seems we are," he rasped. "Is that okay?"

Before she could answer, the shop door opened behind them, signaled with the jangle of the bell.

Lori stepped back and picked up the ribbon and scissors again, as if she hadn't just been turning his world upside down.

"Hi, Mrs. Rudd," she said to the person who'd just entered. "Can I help you find something?"

"I'm looking for kitchen towels," the woman said. "What do you have with a Thanksgiving design? I can't find the ones I had last year."

"Oh, we have them right over here." Lori squeezed Malcom's hand as she brushed past him.

He busied himself looking through a shelf of candles, pretending to be a customer. When in truth, he couldn't wait for the customer to leave so he could have Lori to himself again.

# Seventeen

LORI DIDN'T KNOW WHAT TO think about what was developing between her and Malcom as she waited for him to drive his truck across the street. She could very well walk over to his trailer, but he'd said he'd pick her up. Kissing him last night had been . . . really amazing. And this afternoon, in the shop? That kiss had taken things to another level. First, it was in a public place, which was kind of a declaration in and of itself. And it had been in the middle of the day, and not after some romantic date. So another declaration.

Malcom seemed to be the kind of guy who didn't wait if he wanted something. He simply acted.

And now, Lori's cheeks were hot again.

What *were* they doing, though? Malcom didn't know his plans from one day to the next, and Lori . . . well, she wasn't going to allow herself to finally crush on a guy, only to have him disappear. She needed to focus on things that she knew were guarantees. Like prepping her parents' house to sell and planning the expansion of her shop.

Her phone rang. It was her mom, of course, of all the moments. "Hello?"

"You were right about the postal scam," her mother said.

"I talked to my neighbor, and she said her husband had clicked on some weird link, and then his phone went haywire."

Lori was barely listening because she saw a truck pull up in front of her shop. *Malcom.*

"Oh that's too bad about your neighbor. Look, Mom, I'll call you later, if that's okay," she said in a rush. "I'm heading to Everly's for dinner."

"Oh? A girls' night out?"

"Not exactly." Lori balanced her phone against her shoulder and picked up the casserole dish that was still warm. She headed toward the shop door, but paused before opening it. "It's the girls and the guys. But I'm running late."

Not late quite yet, but there was the risk of that. Not that she couldn't be a little late. She tried to balance the casserole dish with one hand and open the door, but it really needed to be carried with two hands.

"Who's your plus one?" her mom asked.

"What?" Lori gritted her teeth. She'd said too much. "Uh, my friend Malcom."

And now he was out of the truck. Probably seeing that she was having a bit of difficulty.

"I've asked around about him—" her mom started.

"What do you mean you asked around?"

"Well, I talked to Lydia, and she said—"

The door opened, and Malcom was suddenly standing there. "Need an extra hand or two?" he asked.

"Is that him?" Her mom's voice came through loud and clear. "Maybe I can say hello?"

"You're not saying hello," Lori bit out, then regretted her sharp tone. It would only be another thing to apologize for. Besides, Malcom could hear everything.

She handed the casserole dish to him, then grasped her phone. "Look, I'll call you later. Love you." She hung up before her mom could reply. "Sorry about that."

When she looked up at Malcom, he only smiled. "I'd be happy to say hello to your mom."

Lori huffed out a breath. "Don't you dare."

His brows shot up. "Dare what? Speak to your mom?"

She waved a hand at his person. "Be all amazing and stuff. My mom will be making wedding plans before you can hang up with her." She turned to lock the shop door, giving her flaming cheeks a moment to cool off.

His chuckle was low. "She sounds like an entertaining person."

"Oh, she is." A text buzzed her phone, and Lori glanced at it. "Speaking of my mom, she's now texting me. Wants to know where you grew up."

Malcom's eyes creased with his smile. "Tell her Montana."

Lori put her phone on silent. "I think she can wait. How about we change the subject?" She crossed to the truck, and Malcom barely made it in time to open the door for her. She climbed into the passenger seat. "I'll just hold the casserole on my lap, so it doesn't slide around."

Malcom set the dish on her lap after she put on her seat belt.

When he climbed into the other side of the truck, he paused before pulling out onto the road. "How are you?"

She released a slow exhale. "Fine. How are you?" How did he do that? Amid all the chaos, a simple question made her feel seen and noticed by him.

"I'm great," he said, putting on his blinker. "The rest of my afternoon has been kind of crazy, but I'm hoping it's all going to lead to some great stuff."

Now Lori was curious. "Like what?"

He glanced over at her as they reached a stop sign where they'd turn left. "I want to bid for the condo project," he said. "Take it over. I'm lining up investors. Austin is interested, he said. And there are a few others too. If I can get the final person on board, then I should be able to qualify for a bank loan."

Lori stared at him. Austin was going to invest and . . . "You're going to take it over from your brother?"

He smiled over at her, then turned onto the next road. "Essentially. I mean, he's off the project because of his bankruptcy, so I'll be approaching the city again. But I'm pretty sure the mayor will be happy to have my offer so quickly. We can start up again as soon as the bank approves it."

"Wow." Lori wasn't sure what she felt. She was impressed, that was for sure, but it was more than that. A fluttering had started deep in her belly. "So you're sticking around if that approval goes through?"

"I'm sticking around no matter what," Malcom said, his voice low, soft. "Austin offered me a foreman job at the museum if my plan doesn't happen." He slowed the truck in front of Everly and Austin's home. Light spilled out onto the porch and steps, and cars filled the driveway.

Malcom wasn't leaving—at least not this year. Would he stick around after his job was done? Regardless, he needed these good things to happen, especially after how his brother betrayed him.

"That's really amazing, Malcom," she said as he pulled to a stop. "Everyone will be so excited."

"Are you?" he asked, his gaze focused on her, his eyes dark in the cab of the truck.

"Of course I'm excited," she admitted. "And I'm so happy for you. I hope you get that loan."

"Me too." He didn't move.

She didn't move. Were they going to keep sitting here? And why did it feel like butterflies were swarming inside of her?

"I was wondering . . ." he began. "Since we have all this

good news happening, maybe you might reconsider our dating status?"

She swallowed as the butterflies pushed their way into her throat. "You mean beyond you kissing me in random places?"

He chuckled. "Yes, beyond that. You don't have to answer me now," he said. "In fact, take your time to think about it, since I'm not going anywhere."

*Ever? Or just for a while?*

"Okay, I'll think about it." Did she really have to think about it? It might be a good idea to take some time, because at this moment, she wanted to tug him closer and kiss him. But if she did that, it would be written all over her face, and her friends would surely notice.

He leaned over and kissed her cheek, lingering for a moment. "Did I tell you that I like you?"

"You said you liked my earrings."

He drew away. "That's true too." He opened his door and climbed out. Just like that.

Lori was trying to decide if she was disappointed he hadn't kissed her for real, when he opened her door and lifted the casserole dish off her lap.

"Ready?" he asked, his gaze locked on hers.

It seemed that he was asking more than if she was ready to head into Everly's house. "Yes."

"You beat us," Brandy's voice sang from a car that slowed behind the truck. "Looks like you brought something substantial."

"A casserole," Lori said.

Ian turned off the engine, and he and Brandy climbed out of the car.

"We brought chips and salsa," she said. "Boring, I know, but we both ended up having extra busy days." She eyed Malcom.

Lori looked from him to Brandy. What was going on?

"You might as well spill it," Ian said, coming around the car and draping an arm over Brandy's shoulders. "You know you're dying to."

"Spill what?" Lori asked.

"Only if it's okay with Malcom," Brandy said coyly.

"It's okay," he said in a steady voice.

*Huh?* Lori was completely lost.

"Ian is going to invest in the condo project with Malcom," Brandy blurted with a huge smile.

Lori's brain jogged to catch up. "Oh. Wow. That's great."

Ian grinned. "The numbers line up, and I'm also going to build furniture for the main office lobby. A little publicity on my part."

Warmth prickled Lori's arms. If Ian was investing, and Austin was too, it meant that Malcom was really entrenching himself into Everly Falls. Which made her both exhilarated and nervous at the same time. What if they did date, and it didn't work out? Would their friends have to choose sides?

She brushed that thought away because Everly had just opened the door to the house. "Well, come in, everyone." She waved an arm full of jangling bracelets. "The party's inside, not out in the dark."

Everyone headed inside, and the conversation about Ian investing was put on hold. Lori had more questions, but here and now weren't the right place and time. Was Ian the final person he'd been waiting on? No, she decided. Malcom hadn't seemed surprised.

Everly and Austin had set up a long table in their living room so everyone could be seated together.

"Love your outfit," Stephenie said, coming over for a hug.

"I love yours too," Lori said.

Stephenie was wearing a dress, of course—a dark red one

that paired well with her deep-brown knee-length boots. Lori's light sweater was embroidered with the outlines of autumn leaves, which also went with her silver earrings in the same leaf shape.

Malcom set the casserole dish on the table, then fell into a conversation with Austin and Cal as Austin explained some of the upgrades he'd done on this older home.

With Malcom so thoroughly occupied, Lori felt like she should be doing something so she wouldn't just follow him around like she wanted to. She headed into the kitchen, where the women had congregated.

"What can I do to help?" she asked Everly.

"He is sooo into you," Brandy said in a hushed whisper from where she was pouring salsa into a glass bowl. "And I think it's cute that he carried the casserole in."

Lori had to stop from rolling her eyes. "Cute? He was helping."

Brandy just grinned, matching Everly's smile. The sisters both looked like Cheshire cats.

"I must say I agree." Julie paused in adding dressing to a giant green salad. "Dave saw him at the bank today and said that Malcom brought you up several times."

Lori frowned. "What did he say?"

She waved a hand. "I don't know. Men don't elaborate." She glanced toward the living room as if to make sure they weren't being spied upon. "But the fact that Dave even mentioned it . . . that's significant." She waggled her eyebrows.

Should Lori tell her friends about what Malcom had said in the truck? Ask for their advice?

"What's going on?" Brandy asked. "I know that look—something's up."

Lori released a breath and took a seat at the counter on one of the stools. "If I tell you, you have to promise not to say a word—and that means to any of the guys. And especially your *mom*, Brandy and Everly."

The sisters exchanged surprised looks.

"Cross my heart," Brandy said, doing just that.

The men's voices rumbled from the front room, something about shelves.

But Lori lowered hers just the same. "He wants to officially date."

Her friends squealed, keeping their voices down. Still, Lori's eyes widened as she panicked that they'd been overheard. But there didn't seem to be a break in the men's conversation.

"I'm so happy for you," Brandy said, clapping her hands silently.

Lori held up her hand though. "I haven't given him an answer yet. I mean, I don't know how long he'll be in Everly Falls."

Everly came around the counter and set a hand on her shoulder. "I think he's made it pretty obvious he's staying."

"Really?" Julie asked, eyes wide. "I thought his job had been nixed."

Stephenie elbowed her as Austin and Cal walked into the kitchen.

"Need help with anything?" Austin asked.

"You can grab the drinks," Everly said. "We'll carry the rest in."

Lori pulled out her phone and sent a text to the group. *I'll explain more later.*

They all gathered at the table, then began to pass around the food. The potluck was a success because the food choices seemed to all go together. Maybe not in theme, but Lori's casserole paired well with Julie's salad, the fruit platter from Stephenie, Ian's potato salad, and Austin's peach pie—the only decent thing he could make, he claimed.

Through it all, Lori was hyperaware of everything Malcom. What he said, who he talked to, when he looked at her, when he smiled . . . basically, his very presence. It wasn't really a question if she *wanted* to date this man, it was if she *should.* Because, right now, right here, it seemed the perfect scenario. All of her friends enjoyed being around him. But their hearts weren't on the line—not like hers.

# Eighteen

"That was fun," Malcom said as they pulled away from Everly and Austin's house. Conversations he'd had with the various people still played in his head.

Lori smiled over at him. "I'm glad you had a good time."

He reached for her hand, and she linked their fingers. That was a good sign, right?

He'd held off on any PDA during the evening because he didn't know what her answer would be. And even if she'd told him yes, he didn't know how she felt about PDA. Malcom didn't want to press his luck in any form.

"You have a great group of friends," he said. "You're lucky to have that."

"I am," she agreed. "I should be more grateful more often. I mean, I am grateful, but I also feel like I should be more involved. They do a lot of stuff without me."

"You're kind of busy," he said, rubbing a thumb over her fingers. This was nice. Being a couple. Did she think so too?

Malcom had put his phone on silent all night, and he was sure he had several things to address. Right now, he just wanted to spend more time with Lori—without an audience. But he also wanted to make sure he gave her space. So he said,

"Do you want to catch dinner tomorrow after your shop closes?"

She glanced over at him as they pulled onto the road leading to her shop. "I'll have to play it by ear tomorrow. I'm working at my parents' house, then I need to get ready for Turkey Day."

"What's Turkey Day?"

"It's like a Thanksgiving Fair at the community center," she said. "I'm doing a booth this year. We're hosting a craft, and I'll hand out holiday shopping coupons."

"I'm happy to help with any of it."

Lori looked at him in surprise. "You don't need to—I mean, you have so much going on." She paused. "Did you leave your trailer door open?"

"What?" Malcom frowned and glanced over at his trailer as he pulled up alongside the curb in front of Lori's shop. Across the way, he could see lights blazing inside the trailer, and sure enough, the door was open. Wide open. "That's weird. I didn't leave on any lights either."

"Something's wrong," Lori said quietly.

Malcom felt it too. Something wasn't right.

"We should call the police," she continued.

But he shook his head. "It could be one of the construction crew. Maybe I didn't lock the door. They came in to ask questions, and forgot to shut the door after leaving."

"Let's hope it's that innocent," she said. "I'm coming with you to check it out."

If Malcom was wrong, he didn't want Lori going into the trailer. He had no idea what he'd find. "I'll go check it out, then call you. You stay here."

"Malcom, I'm coming," she said, her voice firm.

He met her steady gaze. "Let's drive over, and you stay in the truck while I go inside. Okay?"

He saw her waver, but she agreed.

By the time he drove the short distance, his pulse was pounding. *It's fine,* he told himself. Just someone forgot to shut the door. He'd probably left it unlocked even though he always double-checked before going anywhere.

Leaving Lori in the truck, he headed toward the trailer. Before he even stepped inside, he could see the destruction, and his heart sank to the floor.

Malcom walked through the trailer in a daze. The place had been ransacked, or more accurately, destroyed. Not only were his files upended and scattered, but his laptop was missing. The drawers of his desk were pulled out and overturned. The bathroom, the bedroom, and the small kitchen had all been searched. Nothing had been left unturned. Even the bedding and his clothing had been rifled through.

He had no idea what all was missing in addition to the laptop and probably a bunch of reports. Was this a disgruntled crew member? Or maybe Bronson? As much as Malcom hated to think that his brother would stoop so low, he wasn't sure of anything anymore.

"Malcom?" he heard Lori say.

"Back here," he said.

She appeared in the doorway of the bedroom, her face pale, her eyes wide with disbelief. "This is crazy." She brought a hand to her heart, and her eyes filled with tears. "Who would do this to you?"

He crossed the room and pulled her into his arms. "I don't know."

Lori wrapped her arms about him, holding him tight. "Don't touch anything," she whispered. "We need to call the police and let them search for evidence and fingerprints."

"Okay," he breathed. After a long moment, Malcom released her and made the phone call. The few minutes it took for them to show up felt like the longest minutes in his life. But he had Lori at his side. With his permission, she let her friends know, and they all offered a place for him to stay that night.

"Or you can stay at my place with me and Tiger," Lori said, after the police had filled out their report and allowed him to take some of his personal belongings before they cordoned everything off. "It's your choice."

"If you don't mind me crashing on your couch," he said. "Then tomorrow I can figure where I'll be staying."

"Sure, I mean, it *is* a nice couch." She smiled tentatively.

He smiled back, even though his life was literally in shambles all around him. "It is."

Once they reached Lori's apartment, Malcom was momentarily distracted by Tiger, who seemed to know he needed a buddy. The kitten crawled up his shirt and nestled against his neck, purring.

"You have a fan," Lori said, setting her laptop on the table.

The police had told him to change all of his passwords since the thief could probably access anything he wasn't logged out of. So he spent the next hour changing passwords on everything. Thankfully the verifications all came to his cell phone. He logged into his bank account to see if anything had been transferred or withdrawn, but everything looked like it was in place. In the morning, he'd buy another laptop and download everything from the cloud.

"I'm glad I had my wallet with me," he said. "One less thing to worry about."

"I can't believe this happened to you—after so much already," Lori said. "Do you have any idea who it was?"

"I know what you're thinking," Malcom said. "But I don't think it was my brother. He already has access to company records."

"Won't his assets be frozen though?" Lori asked. "Would

that motivate him to search through your stuff for any loopholes?"

Malcom rubbed a hand over his forehead. "I don't know," he said. "I sent him a text, but he hasn't replied."

"You texted him to ask if he broke into the trailer?"

"Not in those words," he said. "I just said I had my laptop stolen and if he knew anything about it."

"He might not be happy to be accused—that is if he's innocent."

He exhaled. "Yeah. I know, but everything's messed up anyway. What's one more accusation?"

Lori reached over and grasped his hand. He turned his palm up and linked their fingers. "Thanks for letting me crash here. And for everything else."

"No problem," she said, her voice soft. "I mean it. I just wish I had an extra bed for you, so you'd be more comfortable." Her eyes glimmered with amusement.

"We could share," he teased.

"I'm not that generous of a host," she said. "We're not even dating."

He chuckled. "Let me know when you want to change that."

"I think you have enough going on, without having a relationship talk."

"Speak for yourself." He drew her hand toward him. "Come here."

She rose from her chair, and he tugged her onto his lap. He liked her closer. She smiled and looped her arms about his neck. He liked how she fit against him.

"You smell like peaches and cinnamon," he said.

"Probably Austin's pie. You smell the same."

"Hmm. Have you thought about my question from earlier?"

She tilted her head. "About dating? That one?"

"Yep."

Lori traced her fingers over his shoulder, then down his arm. His skin heated at her touch. "I just worry about how long you'll be in Everly Falls."

Malcom blinked. Had he not made it clear? He was here to stay—if that was all right with her. "I don't have plans to go anywhere else. Unless you kick me out."

The edges of her mouth turned up. "As if..."

"So... is that a yes?"

Her shoulders shifted as she edged closer. "It's a yes."

"I think that's the best news I've heard all day."

"That wasn't hard to do considering the day you've had."

He chuckled, then kissed her softly, slowly. When she angled her mouth against his, he took it deeper, breathing in peaches and cinnamon. He really needed to get that pie recipe from Austin.

His heart was thudding loud enough that Lori could probably hear it. "I'm really glad you said yes," he murmured against her mouth.

She smiled and tightened her hold on him.

When his phone rang, he ignored it at first, then realized it was probably important. Maybe even the police.

He drew away from Lori and reached for it.

She moved off his lap as he answered. "Bill Jennings, how are you?" he asked. Bill ran Jennings Carpets and he'd been interested in investing.

"Hi, Malcom," Bill said through the phone. "I saw police cars at the building lot tonight—is everything all right?"

"My trailer was ransacked," Malcom said. "Got my laptop stolen, and I've been busy changing all the passwords."

"Oh boy, that's terrible," Bill said. "Any idea who broke in?"

"I don't, but the police are working on it." Malcom glanced over at Lori. "I'll be sticking around in Everly Falls though, so I'm finding a more permanent place tomorrow anyway. One with better security."

"There's a basement apartment for rent in my neighborhood," Bill said. "If you're interested?"

"Sure, send along the address," he said. "I'll check it out."

"Are you still looking to take over the condo project?"

Malcom straightened at this. "Yes, definitely. I'm meeting with the bank as soon as I have the investors lined up."

Bill cleared his throat. "Well, I'm calling to tell you that I'm in. I'd like to invest. I went over this with my wife, and she's excited as well."

Malcom fist-pumped the air. "Excellent. That's great news. When you have a chance, just sign and send over the agreement I gave you. I'm very much looking forward to working with you."

"Me too," Bill said. "You're a good man for doing this, Malcom."

When he hung up, Lori was staring at him expectantly. "Bill Jennings is the final investor that I needed." He couldn't help but grin. "Looks like I'm going to the bank in the morning. Right after I get a laptop."

"Wow, that's amazing. Truly." Lori hugged him, and he pulled her onto his lap for another kiss. Plenty of doors had shut on him the past week, but he was grateful for all of the windows that had opened.

# Nineteen

*SO... WHAT DID YOU TELL Malcom about your decision to date him?* Brandy texted first thing the next morning.

*Yeah, we're on pins and needles here,* Everly added.

*Aren't any of you working this morning?* Lori wrote back.

Her mom had also called, but she let that go to voicemail because she'd been in the middle of painting the living room of her parents' old house. Now, she was taking a short break. She'd replied to Malcom's texts, of course. He'd started the morning early, buying a laptop in town and then heading to the bank. When the meeting was over, he'd texted her: *All I can do now is wait.*

Then he said he'd be looking around town for a place to stay.

Lori didn't tell him to rush because she liked having him at her place, but maybe for that very reason, he needed to find somewhere soon. Everyone he'd talked to had suggestions.

*We're officially dating,* Lori wrote her friend group. *But stay off my back about it. We're taking things really slowly. Like slower than a snail.* Well, they were mostly taking things slowly, except for spending every spare minute together.

*That might change if he keeps crashing at your place,* Stephenie wrote.

Julie added some laughing emojis, then wrote, *Ah, young love*.

Her phone rang, jarring Lori from her smile. Mom, again.

"There you are," her mother said when she picked up. "I've been trying you all morning."

"I've been painting," Lori said in a patient voice. Her mom had tried *once*, and hadn't left a voicemail, so it shouldn't be urgent, right?

"Oh, that's nice," her mother said in a conciliatory tone, obviously not all that interested. "Lydia told me that Malcom Graves's trailer was broken into last night."

Lori pinched her eyes shut. How did her mom find out things so fast? Oh, that's right, talking to Lydia.

She continued without waiting for any sort of reply. "Is that what Everly Falls is coming to? I knew that larger developments would bring in more crime. Lydia told me that the project has stalled. Do you know anything about that?"

"It's only temporary—" Lori began.

"I don't know if this man is who you think he is, Lori. Do you really think you should be spending time with—"

"Mom," she cut in. "You need to listen to me and stop gossiping with friends who don't know what's really going on."

"I'm not—"

"You *are*. If you want to know the truth, then listen. If you don't, then hang up and go about your day, doing whatever you've planned."

Silence on the other end told Lori that she'd truly shocked her mom.

"I'm listening," she finally said in a plaintive tone.

Lori gave her mom the bird's-eye view of what had happened with Malcom's brother, and how he was now putting together a plan to take over the condo project on his own.

"Oh my goodness," her mom said, her voice filled with

awe. "That poor man. I can't imagine going through that betrayal."

"He's a stalwart guy," Lori said. "Has a good head on his shoulders and really cares about Everly Falls and the community. And I'm dating him, Mom, so you're hearing it straight from me. No need to call up your gossipy friends."

Her mom squealed. "You're finally dating someone? You should bring him for Thanksgiving. He probably doesn't want to be around his family anyway."

Lori laughed. "You're probably right. But Thanksgiving is kind of a big deal. I mean, you're in Florida."

"You already have your ticket," Mom said. "See what he says."

Lori wasn't sure about inviting Malcom for a weekend with her parents. Things were really new between them, and she had no idea what the next couple of weeks might bring with the condo project. Maybe everything would fall through. Or maybe he'd be busier than ever.

After finally getting off the phone with her mom, Lori felt drained of energy. She grabbed the lunch she'd packed and checked in with Marci to see how the store was doing. Marci said it had been busy, but nothing she couldn't keep up with.

When Lori heard a truck rumble in front of the house, then come to a stop, she crossed to the window. To her surprise, Malcom and two other men climbed out—Austin and Cal. They walked up the driveway and crossed to the porch.

She reached the door just as one of them knocked. Opening it, she said, "What's going on?"

Then she noticed they all carried tools.

"We're here to help," Malcom said, his hazel eyes landing on hers.

"I . . . I wasn't expecting anyone."

Last night, she'd told Malcom about some of the projects that had to be done on the house after painting. She hadn't intended to make him feel like she needed *his* help. She had all winter to get the house ready.

But apparently, he'd shown up anyway.

"I'll start painting," Cal said. "Wore my painting shirt."

Lori laughed. His faded blue T-shirt did look like it had been through several painting projects. "Grab a roller, then."

"I can install the kitchen fixtures," Austin said, walking past her, toolbox in hand.

Malcom stepped into the house last, but before he could move too far inside, Lori placed a hand on his chest. "You don't have time for this."

His warm eyes searched hers, his mouth lifting into a half smile. "I always have time for you."

She felt her eyes burn, and she blinked rapidly. "How did you talk the others into this?"

"Turns out they had a slow day."

Lori smirked. She very much doubted that, but her heart swelled with gratitude. "Thank you."

"You're welcome."

She raised up on her toes and kissed him. She didn't care who saw, either.

For the next several hours, the house was filled with the sounds of drilling and hammering, as fixtures were installed, the paint in the living room completed, the linoleum in the kitchen and bathrooms torn up, and the carpet in the bedrooms removed.

Malcom had talked her into new flooring. Said that with his contractor's discount on supplies, the cost would be much less than putting a carpet or flooring allowance into the buyers' contract.

Lori had argued that most of the savings came from the

labor, but Malcom said he'd only charge if he needed someone to help.

"You can lay flooring?" she asked. Of course he could, but did he have time for it?

"It's easy, and kind of fun," he said. "You could even help."

"Oh, I'll help."

They were standing in the hallway, now stripped of carpet, and Malcom had his hands on her hips. Lori rested her hands on his shoulders, his sleeves damp with perspiration. She didn't mind Malcom sweaty in the least.

"You're doing too much," she said, in a last-ditch effort.

"*You're* doing too much," he countered.

She was pretty sure he was going to kiss her, but Austin's voice broke in from the front room. "The carpet's all loaded into the back of the truck. Anything else we need to haul away?"

Lori stepped out of Malcom's arms just as Austin came around the corner.

"Oh, sorry," he said with an innocent smile. "Didn't mean to interrupt."

"It's fine," Malcom said, joining him in the living room. Lori followed. "How far is the local dump?"

"About fifteen minutes." Austin wiped at his sweaty brow.

"Should I drop you and Cal off first?" Malcom asked.

"Nah," Austin said. "We'll come and help unload. You can buy us dinner."

"Sounds good." Malcom said with a chuckle.

"I should be paying for your dinner," she cut in.

"I've got it." Malcom flashed a smile. "You could come with us, though."

"I wish. I'm going to tape the kitchen in prep for painting, then head back to the store and help Marci close up."

Malcom nodded.

"When are you putting this place on the market?" Austin asked.

"Next spring? You want to buy it and flip it?" she asked, half-teasing, but curious also.

"I was just thinking that maybe Malcom could rent the place from you," he said. "You know, so it's not vacant all that time."

"But it's in shambles," Lori said. "Even before you guys showed up to tear out flooring and replace fixtures, the place was not livable."

Austin shrugged. "He could throw down a mattress, and as long as the bathroom is working?"

Lori looked over at Malcom, expecting him to say he'd prefer other options. But he stood with his hands on his hips, looking about the place. "We could work out a trade," he said in a thoughtful tone. "My handiwork in exchange for rent. Or I could outright pay rent. Whatever your parents want—that is, if you need their permission?"

"They'd probably be fine with it," Lori said slowly. "I mean, more than fine. But you don't have time to renovate a house in exchange for rent. You could stay here for free. I should have thought about it before. I just don't think it's all that livable."

"Like Austin said, it has a working bathroom. And I'm assuming the furnace will kick on when it gets colder outside?"

"It works." Lori huffed out a breath. "Maybe think about it. It would be a big change."

"An upgrade from my trailer," he said with a laugh. "I'm good with it if you're good with it."

Lori gazed at him for a moment, then glanced at Austin. Malcom really was planning on staying . . . it wasn't until this moment that it truly sank in.

"I'm fine with it too," she admitted.

"Great." Malcom grinned. "I'll move in tonight."

And just like that, it was settled. Just like that, Lori's life had taken another turn. She stood on the porch as she watched Malcom's truck pull away with Cal and Austin, the truck bed full of torn-up flooring. What was happening to her life?

She stepped back inside to call her parents and tell them they now had a renter.

"That's wonderful," her mom gushed over the phone after being updated on how much work had been done today. "Dad's golfing right now, but I'll tell him as soon as he returns. I'm sure he'll want to add to the list of repairs."

"I'm still going to be doing as much as I can myself," Lori said. "Malcom has a lot going on right now, so I'm not going to give him a giant list."

Her mother chuckled. "He seems to really like you, Lori. I'm so happy about that. Is he coming for Thanksgiving?"

"I haven't asked him yet," she said. *Would* she ask him? Her pulse sped up at the thought. Bringing him to meet her parents felt very . . . official.

After hanging up with her mom, she texted her friend group about Malcom moving in. She wanted to pay back some of his kind deeds. *Moving party tonight for those who can make it. Malcom's going to rent my parents' house. I'll order some pizzas.*

*What???* Brandy wrote back. *You're kidding me! Let me pick up my jaw off the floor.*

*It's just practical. Austin suggested it,* Lori said. *No need to flip out.*

Brandy sent a GIF of a gymnast doing a floor routine.

*My husband's a genius,* Everly wrote, adding heart eyes.

*Cal and I will be there,* Stephenie texted. *Can't wait.*

*I'll find a sitter,* Julie wrote. *Should be fun.*

*Thanks, everyone,* Lori added. *I'll let you know the exact time when it gets closer.*

She set down her phone and climbed up on the stepladder. As she began to tape the edge of the kitchen cupboards with painter's tape, she felt, for the first time in a long time, she was not a third wheel—or a fifth wheel. She was looking forward to everyone hanging out together, everyone helping Malcom, a man who was becoming more and more important to her. And she didn't mind who knew it.

# Twenty

It was true that many hands made light work. Malcom was pretty sure his moving stint had broken all moving records in history. He stood in one of the back bedrooms, surveying the work.

The bed was set up, and his desk. He'd brought over the furniture he'd collected over the years—even though nothing really matched. He'd worry about that stuff when he had a more permanent place one day. In a corner sat a stack of boxes that he'd dumped all the files in—out of order for now. He still didn't know the extent of the damage from the break-in the other night.

For now, he could live here and get his business up and running.

"Are you hungry?" Lori asked, coming into the room.

When the pizza was delivered, everyone had congregated in the kitchen, where conversation and laughter came from now. But Malcom wanted to finish stacking the file boxes.

He looked over at her. She wore a T-shirt that said *Be Thankful*, and well-worn jeans. He was impressed how she gathered all her friends to help him move. It wasn't a big job or hard job, but he appreciated the help and support.

"I am hungry," he said.

Lori smiled that beautiful smile of hers. "Then what are you waiting for? Come and eat."

Malcom walked toward her. "I was just appreciating how my girlfriend is taking care of me."

Her brows lifted. "Oh, I'm your girlfriend now?"

"If you want to be." He stopped right in front of her, nearly toe to toe.

She looped her arms about his neck. "Let's see how this dating thing goes first."

"You're already messing with my heart," he said close to her ear as he settled his hands about her waist.

"Hmm," she murmured, her warm breath a flutter against his skin. "What are your plans for Thanksgiving?"

This surprised him, and he drew back. Thanksgiving was coming up, but it had been the last thing on his mind, despite thinking of the holiday every time he saw Lori.

"I think I've been uninvited to my brother's, and you couldn't pay me to go to my mom's—uh, my parents."

Lori moved her fingers into his hair. "Well, I have a backup plan if you need it."

"I need it."

Her mouth lifted into a smile, and he was about to kiss her when she said, "Come with me to Florida. My mom is dying to meet you. My dad too, although he won't admit it. You could talk about tools together."

Malcom smirked. "Tools? I'm sure that will take at least a whole day's conversation."

"It is what it is," she said with a shrug.

"I think I'd love to go to Florida to talk about tools with your dad," he said, then brushed his lips against her cheek. "Will there be food too?"

"Of course there will be food." She turned her face so that the next brush of his lips made contact with her own.

Malcom drew her closer, bringing their bodies flush as they continued to kiss. Someone laughed in the other room. Sounded like everyone was enjoying themselves, but he didn't want to move away from Lori.

When she drew back, her lips were redder and her cheeks pink. "We should join the others, or they'll wonder what's going on."

"What is going on, Lori?" he asked, lifting a hand and touching the stud earrings in her ears in the shape of little teacups. "I think going to your parents' for Thanksgiving puts us at boyfriend-girlfriend status."

Lori gave a little shrug. "We'll see. It might just be tool talk." She drew away and stepped out of his arms, but he grasped her hand before she could get too far.

"Let's go out tomorrow night. Dinner somewhere. Just us. As much as I like your friends, I'm feeling selfish when it comes to you."

"They're your friends now too," Lori corrected.

"Our friends," Malcom amended. "You pick a place."

She turned more fully toward him. "Okay. I guess we're really going to date, then?"

"You did invite me to Thanksgiving."

"True."

He leaned down for another kiss, which was over way too quick. Because apparently Lori had an agenda to get him fed for the night. "Okay, I'll think of a place," she said, then drew him out of the room with a hand.

Once everyone ate and took off, Malcom drove Lori back to her apartment. "Thanks again," he said, as they turned onto the street.

"Did you leave the trailer lights on?" Lori asked.

Malcom noticed the lights just as she spoke. He knew he hadn't because he'd purposely turned them off now that the place was empty. Tomorrow, a semi would haul it off the lot and to wherever Bronson wanted it. He had yet to reply to Malcom's text about it. Ironic that his brother should ghost *him*.

He turned toward the trailer. "That's Penny's car." Adrenaline shot through him. What was she doing here? He hadn't talked to her since the blowup with Bronson. "Maybe she's going to handle where the trailer is going since Bronson hasn't answered me."

"Should we call the cops?" Lori asked.

"I don't know yet," Malcom said truthfully. He wasn't afraid of Penny, but who knew what she would do. The cops still didn't know who'd ransacked his place.

"Wait here," he said as he parked the truck.

"I'm not waiting in the truck while you face that terrible woman," Lori said, and opened her door before Malcom could say anything else.

She grasped his hand as they headed toward the trailer.

Malcom's heart thumped hard—he had no idea what to expect. When he opened the door, he found Penny inside, leaning against the counter, talking on the phone.

The instant she saw him, she straightened. "I need to go, Bronson." She clicked off and stared at him, then her gaze moved to Lori.

"You're still with her?" Penny said in a steely tone. "I thought she'd be temporary." Her gaze bore into Lori. "Congratulations, honey, you've made it about ten times longer than I predicted."

"Penny," Malcom cut in. "What are you doing here?"

"Returning this," Penny said, holding up his laptop.

"You took it?" he asked, disbelief pulsing through him. Was he really surprised, though?

"No, it was dropped off at Bronson's house," she said.

Malcom narrowed his eyes. Did Penny really expect him to believe that? "Like on the porch? The driveway? Or did the thief ring the doorbell?"

Penny shrugged. "What does it really matter? Your laptop's back, and I decided to be nice and deliver it. Some thanks I'm getting . . ." She looked around the empty trailer. "Where did all your stuff go?"

Malcom pinched the bridge of his nose, trying to figure out what was really going on. He picked up his laptop from the counter. No charging cord, of course. "I don't know what to think," he said stiffly. "My place was ransacked, and suddenly you show up with my stolen property."

"Here." Penny ignored his statement and handed over a stapled set of papers. "We need you to sign this."

Malcom hesitated, then took the papers from her. Leafing through them, he surmised that he'd just been given a nondisclosure, noncompete, and promise-not-to-sue document. Ridiculous. He held out the contract to her. "Send it to my lawyer. Bronson's lawyer has his information."

Penny refused to take it back. She set her hands on her hips. "Seriously, Malcom? This is your own brother. He's working day and night to save everyone's necks, including yours." She pointed a long fingernail at Lori. "It's *her*, isn't it? The minute we start a project in Every Falls, all of a sudden, you're dating a local girl. She and the whole town are in on this together—everyone knows everyone here. Like they're all cousins. So weird. This woman has influenced you to turn your back on your family."

Malcom opened his mouth to respond, but Lori cut in.

"You have thirty seconds to leave this trailer before I call the cops," she said in a dead-calm voice. "Oh, and by the way, the chief of police is my dad's cousin, and I've already sent him the video I just took of you inside this trailer."

Penny gaped at her. "You're a first-rate—"

Malcom stepped in front of Lori just as Penny lunged. Her claws—nails—landed on his chest. He staggered back a step, but managed to remain upright.

That's when they all heard police sirens.

"Move, Malc!" Penny screeched. "This woman is mine!"

He grabbed her arms as she lunged again. "Stop, Penny. You're making everything worse. Do you want assault added to your breaking-and-entering charges?"

Her chest heaved with anger. "This trailer belongs to the company. A company that you're no longer a part of."

"And it's leaving the property tomorrow. A fact which Bronson already knows. You shouldn't have come here, Penny. You shouldn't have taken my laptop," he added. Because suddenly he knew. Being this close to her reminded him of her expensive perfume. He'd caught a whiff of it when he was loading the papers into the boxes earlier tonight. But he'd brushed it off as being his imagination. Now, he realized she'd been the one to go through all his stuff.

"What were you hoping to find?" he ground out.

Penny jerked her arms away from his grasp, rubbing them. "The bankruptcy is all your fault, you know," she hissed. "We were all on our way to being wealthy. I even laid myself at your feet and was willing to create a future together."

The sirens cut off, and red and blue lights glowed against the white blinds.

"What does that even mean?" he asked. "You were going to frame me if things went south?"

Penny scrunched up her face. "You're the one who made the mistakes, not me, not my sister, and not Bronson. Someday, you'll pay for all of this."

Someone banged on the door, and Lori opened it up before the police could bust in.

The next few minutes were a whirlwind as Penny proclaimed her innocence, but the cops insisted they talk to her separately, outside of the trailer.

After they were done with her, one of the cops came back inside. "Do you want to press charges, sir?"

Malcom scrubbed a hand through his hair. It was complicated, but Penny had literally stolen his property.

"This has to end," Lori said quietly.

He nodded, then looked at the cop. "Yes, I do."

# Twenty-One

LORI STOOD AT THE KITCHEN window, which gave her a view of the building lot. Three days ago, the work had resumed. After what seemed like a series of miracles, and brilliant planning by Malcom—plus an approved construction loan—the condo project was back on schedule. It was a little strange with the trailer gone from the lot, but it also signaled that life was moving forward.

The tea kettle whistled, and she moved to the stove and turned off the heat. Then she poured hot water into two mugs she'd set aside for hot chocolate. As she stirred scoops of the mix into the mugs, her thoughts shifted to Penny. The charges against her had been dismissed because there hadn't been enough proof that she'd stolen the laptop. Besides, her name was on the company board, so her entering the trailer wasn't considered trespassing, especially since Malcom had moved his stuff out. Regardless of the disappointment that Penny would get away with everything, Lori hoped she had learned her lesson and would stay away from Malcom from now on.

Tiger meowed and trotted to the door at the sound of footsteps coming up the stairs. Malcom knocked, then opened the door. She'd left it unlocked for him. Without turning she could smell the food he'd brought.

"Breakfast?" he asked, his voice a nice low morning rumble.

She smiled, but didn't turn from stirring the hot chocolate. Seconds later, he'd crossed the room and wrapped his arms about her waist. She leaned her back against his chest, and he kissed her neck, then rested his chin on her shoulder.

"Hot chocolate?" he murmured.

"Mm-hmm."

"Are you packed?"

She turned in his arms. "I am. Did you bring a book?"

"For what?" he teased.

They'd already discussed this more than once. "I'm canceling your ticket if you didn't bring a book."

He drew her closer, and she breathed in his clean shower scent. "They don't let other passengers cancel each other's tickets."

She scrunched up her nose. "There's a first time for everything."

He chuckled. Then he moved a hand to cradle her face. "I brought a book, and I know you're going to love it."

"Is it from my list?" She'd told him in order to take a real vacation, he needed to relax and read a book. So they'd decided—well, she'd decided, and he'd agreed—that they'd pick out a book for each other and bring it. They'd reveal their book gifts on the plane. She wasn't taking any chances, though, and gave him her wish list.

"Maybe, maybe not," Malcom said.

Lori frowned. "That doesn't sound promising. I vote that if I don't like the book you got me, then we're going to switch."

"You mean you haven't already read the book you bought me?"

She bit her lip. "I have, but . . ."

Malcom pressed a kiss at the edge of her mouth, his gaze full of amusement. "You'd rather reread a book than trust my judgment?"

She hooked her hands behind his neck and rose up on her toes to kiss him. She wondered if there was anything better than kissing this man in the morning. "I guess we'll just have to wait and see."

The sound of a construction truck rumbled on the other side of the window. "They're starting early," she said. "Are you sure you can leave everything? You just got everything back on track."

"Thanksgiving only comes once a year," Malcom said. "Besides, some of my employees want the extra hours. Otherwise, I'd shut down for the entire holiday."

"You're a good boss," she said, just as Tiger rubbed against their legs, giving a pitiful meow. One that said he'd been neglected far too long.

Malcom released her and bent to pick up the kitten. "The question is: Can you leave this little guy for so long?"

Lori took Tiger in her arms and kissed the top of his furry head. "Marci will take good care of him, and she promised to send me pictures every day."

Malcom shook his head, looking amused again. "As long as you're not video chatting with a cat."

Lori shrugged. "That might happen."

"Are you serious?"

She turned Tiger toward him. "Just look at this cute face. You have to admit, you're going to miss him too."

"Maybe a little, but I really don't need photos from Marci or any video chats."

Lori just smiled. "All right. You do you." She set Tiger down and moved to the table. "What did you bring me?"

"Bagels—hope that's not boring."

"Food is never boring."

As they sat to eat, Lori pushed back the nerves that kept trying to rise. She was excited that Malcom was coming with her to Florida for Thanksgiving. To meet her parents. Yeah, it was definitely a first for her—bringing home a man, so to speak. Though everything was going well with him, better than she had expected or could have ever dreamed, she kept waiting for something to turn her off. Or for him to lose interest. But neither had happened.

Brandy had scolded her last night in a phone call when Lori had admitted to her maudlin thoughts. "Good things can happen to you, Lori. Enjoy the moments. Enjoy the process of falling in love."

Lori wasn't falling in love, no. She was just becoming comfortable, and maybe even confident, when she was around this man. Waking up each morning, and wondering if Malcom would ghost her, and she'd never see him again . . . that hadn't happened yet. And having him in her kitchen this morning felt completely natural. Like they'd been together forever.

As if on cue, her phone started to buzz with incoming texts.

"Your friends all worked up?" Malcom said with a half smile.

Lori smirked and reached for her phone. "Looks like it."

The group text was buzzing with everyone chatting about their Thanksgiving plans. Julie said she was going to have to take anti-anxiety meds to survive the weekend with her in-laws. Everly and Brandy would be doing a big shindig at their mom's, and Everly's in-laws were coming into town for that.

Stephenie and Cal would be serving the dinner at the senior center, dragging her grandpa with them.

*Lori, you're going to have the best time in Florida,* Brandy wrote. *With that hunk of a man charming your parents' socks off.*

Lori sent a laughing emoji.

*I hope Malcom's not too sad about the issues with his family,* Everly chimed in.

That sobered Lori, and she wrote, *It will be a new experience for him, that's for sure.*

"You've gone through like ten different facial expressions in two minutes," Malcom said. "Must be some intense stuff."

Lori looked at him and found his gaze on hers. She set her phone down. "Everyone's excited about our trip—maybe even jealous."

Malcom chuckled. "They're jealous of us flying on the busiest traveling day of the year?"

She smirked. "Everly also said she hopes you're doing okay—you know, with the turmoil of your family and you not having Thanksgiving with them."

His brows shot up. "She said that?"

"Basically."

Malcom didn't speak for a moment. "Is that what you think?"

"Maybe?" Lori shrugged. "You haven't said anything to me, but I do wonder if flying to Florida and being around another person's family will be hard."

"I don't think I've had a normal or traditional Thanksgiving since I was a kid," Malcom said. "If it was ever normal back then. I remember one year my mom ordered Chinese food. She didn't want to cook, and the Chinese restaurant always stayed open on holidays."

She stared at him. "That sounds pretty cool, actually."

Malcom leaned back in his chair. "Another year, my mom was sick, so I opened a can of SpaghettiOs."

Lori blinked. "You didn't have neighbors, or an uncle or aunt to feed you?"

He shook his head. "The first year I lived with my dad and

Bronson, my stepmom invited everyone in her family over. Her brother started talking about politics, which ended up in a shouting match with their other brother."

"Wow." She cracked a smile. "I promise not to talk politics this weekend."

Malcom shifted forward and leaned his elbows on the table. "Wherever you are, that's where I'll be, Lori. I'm not going to worry about what my family might or might not be doing. Believe me, there is no traditional Thanksgiving dinner that I'm pining for. For me, it's about what I'm grateful for in my life, and not the meal or house the meal is in."

Lori exhaled. "You're kind of a poet, Malcom. I mean, if you ever change your mind about building stuff—"

He pushed up from the table and grabbed her, pulling her into his arms. She laughed as he wrapped her into a bear hug.

"Take it back, or I'll keep you trapped like this forever."

She laughed against his neck. "Okay, I take it back. But you can keep me trapped if you want."

The tight hug turned into something that was more of a caress, until Lori said, "We really should leave. I can't wait to see which book you're giving me."

Malcom groaned and released her. "You're such a taskmaster."

Maybe she was, but she also liked to be at the airport in plenty of time. And he was right, it was a crazy day to travel, but by some small miracle, their plane left on time. Once they were in the air, Lori pulled out the wrapped book she'd carried in her purse.

Malcom took his out of the front pocket of the seat, where he'd stored it. "Ready?" he asked with a sly smile.

"Ready."

They swapped wrapped books and opened them at the same time.

Lori laughed as she read the title. "*The Man Who Died Twice.*"

Malcom held up his book. "*The Thursday Murder Club.*"

They were both by the same author, and the same series.

"Are you happy?" he asked, after she stopped laughing. "Or is it corny?"

"It's perfect," she said. "I read the first book, of course, and this book was on my list. You're a smart man." She leaned over and kissed him. The whole plane could know how smart he was.

Malcom grinned. "I think you kissing me on a plane is definitely a girlfriend move."

She slipped her hand into his.

He leaned close to her ear. "And if I thought giving you a book was the way to your heart, I would have done it weeks ago."

She turned her head for another kiss. Yeah, they were going to be *that* couple. "Okay, now be quiet and start reading," she whispered. "We're on vacation."

"I hope we can do more than read," he murmured, then opened to the first page of his book.

Lori was surprised that he actually did start reading, and as he turned pages, her mind was wandering more and more. Butterflies milled around in her stomach as she thought about how this was actually happening. Malcom was going to meet her parents. Maybe it wasn't all that momentous to other people, but for her, it was definitely huge.

She flipped back a couple of pages and started reading from the beginning. She didn't want to miss a single red herring.

"Are we racing?" Malcom asked.

"No, of course not," Lori said, but she noticed that every time she turned a page, he turned a page.

By the time they landed in Florida, they were both over one hundred pages into their books.

Lori texted her parents about arriving—they'd insisted on picking them up.

Malcom turned on his phone as they waited for the aisle to clear in front of them. When his brows tugged together, she asked, "What is it?"

"I need to call my mom," he said. "My dad's in the hospital."

"What? What happened?"

He read the text to her. "'Call me ASAP. Dad's been taken to the hospital. Something with his heart.' She also left a message. And there's a voicemail from Bronson."

Lori met his gaze, seeing the worry there. They both knew Bronson reaching out meant this was a pretty big deal.

They hurried off the plane when it was their turn to head down the aisle, and as they walked into the terminal, Malcom phoned his mom. "She didn't pick up." He shot her a text, then said, "I'll try Bronson."

They paused by a restaurant as he called his brother. Lori could only hear one side of the conversation, but it didn't sound good.

"Surgery? When?"

She frowned.

"Okay. I just landed in Florida." He paused. "With Lori." Another pause. "I'll be there as soon as I can." He clicked off with his brother.

Before he could say anything, Lori asked, "Do you want me to come with you?"

He held her gaze for a moment, and she could see the warring thoughts in his eyes. "I can't ask you to skip Thanksgiving with your parents."

Lori reached for his hand. "There will be other

Thanksgivings. Plus, you said you've never had a normal one anyway, so why start this year?"

One edge of his mouth lifted, but she could see the worry etched in his expression. "I don't really want to be around my family, but now . . ." He swallowed.

"You don't have to explain," Lori said. "They're still your family."

He nodded. "My dad has two blocked arteries and they're putting in stents." He exhaled. "Dad's young enough that he shouldn't have any trouble during surgery or recovery."

"Come on," she said. "Let's go to the airline counter and see which flights are available. Then we can figure out things from there."

"Okay," he said.

As they walked, Lori sent a quick text to her mom, telling her to stay on standby. That they were off the plane, but Malcom had received bad news about his family. A series of questions came in from her, but Lori said she'd explain later.

While waiting in line, Malcom finally got ahold of his mom. "I'm going to try to head there today, so it will probably be tonight. What time is the surgery scheduled for?" When he hung up, he told Lori, "He's going into surgery soon, so by the time I get there, he'll be out."

"It sounds like they're on top of this," Lori said. She finally replied to her mom's texts, telling her the updates and the name of the hospital—because her dad was asking—and that she and Malcom were trying to get tickets to Montana.

When it was their turn at the counter, the only flights they could get that afternoon would take them into other airports too late to catch a connecting flight. They'd have to stay overnight in another city.

"What about flights tomorrow morning?" Malcom asked the service rep. Then he glanced over at Lori. "Are you sure you're okay with this?"

"I'm okay."

So it was arranged that they'd fly out Thanksgiving morning instead.

Lori sent a text to her mom with the latest update. By the time they headed out of the airport, her parents were waiting, and her mom had a plan.

"We're so sorry to hear about your dad," she said, pulling Malcom into a tight hug.

Lori was surprised by the move, and he probably was too.

"I looked up the hospital he's in, and he's in good hands there," her dad said, giving Malcom a firm handshake and a pat on the back.

"We've got all the fixings for dinner already," her mom chimed in, "so we're going to push up the timeline and have dinner tonight. Then we'll get you back to the airport in the morning for your flight."

Lori's eyes filled with tears.

"You're so generous," Malcom said. "I'm sorry about all of this trouble. I didn't mean to show up and throw a wrench into all the plans."

"Nonsense," her mom said. "You're not to blame for anything, and we're just happy to meet someone who's so important to Lori."

Lori might have been a bit embarrassed with her mom saying such things under normal circumstances, but these weren't normal circumstances.

After their carry-ons were loaded into the trunk of her parents' car, she and Malcom climbed into the back seat. Malcom reached for her hand and squeezed. "Thank you," he mouthed.

She could still see the apprehension in his eyes, but he seemed more relaxed now that they had a plan in place. And all they could do was wait for news on the outcome of his dad's surgery.

# Twenty-Two

JUST BEFORE LORI'S MOM ANNOUNCED that dinner was ready—she'd ordered Lori and Malcom to sit out on the deck and relax while watching the sunset—Bronson called.

Malcom pushed to his feet and answered. "Bronson," he said into his phone. "What's the news?"

"Everything went well," Bronson said, his voice sounding relieved. "He's out of surgery, and he's pretty groggy. The doctor said it was all routine as far as stents go, and he should make a full recovery."

Malcom felt like a huge boulder had just rolled off his shoulders. "That's great news." He leaned against the deck railing and released a long breath. "Can I talk to him yet?"

"Maybe in a couple of hours," Bronson said. "Are you still coming?"

He glanced over at Lori, who stood as well and walked to the railing. "Yeah. We fly out in the morning."

"You're bringing Lori?"

The question sounded like one of curiosity, nothing else. "She's coming," Malcom confirmed.

"I think that's great," Bronson said, sincerity in his voice.

Their conversation almost felt normal. As if their

relationship, and their business, hadn't imploded only a few weeks ago. Bronson hadn't brought up Penny, and Malcom was happy not to rehash that disaster again.

"Dad will be happy to see you," he continued, "and everyone wants to meet Lori."

Malcom dragged in a breath. "Yeah . . . Call me or have Mom call me later when I can talk to Dad."

"Will do."

He hung up with Bronson and turned to Lori. "My dad's out of surgery and everything went well."

"Oh, that's great news."

He wiped at his eyes, because apparently his emotions had caught up with him.

Lori wrapped her arms around his waist, and he pulled her close.

"I'm so happy he's okay," she murmured. "It will be good for you to see him in person."

He rested his chin atop her head and closed his eyes. Somehow the universe knew that he needed this woman. "If you want to stay here with your parents, I'd understand."

She only nestled closer. "My parents are great and all, but I'm still coming with you." She drew away slightly and raised her chin to look up at him. "If you're okay with that still?"

He smiled. His first smile in hours. "I'm okay with it. Because, you know, you're my girlfriend."

She smiled at that, and it was a beautiful one. He leaned down and kissed her.

"I hate to interrupt." Her mom's singsong voice came from somewhere by the sliding doors to the deck. "Dinner's ready."

Lori drew back. "Thanks, Mom." She kept her eyes on Malcom. "Ready for the best meal of your life?"

"Ready."

Lori gave a soft laugh, and they entered the house hand in hand.

She was completely right, of course. Her parents were excellent cooks, and they parried off each other, listing what they'd cooked and baked. There was certainly enough food for several more dinner guests.

"We've invited the neighbors over for tomorrow," Mrs. Harding said. "I didn't feel like I should switch them to today, considering what's happening with Malcom's family. We'll just reheat what we need to tomorrow and have giant dinners two nights in a row."

Mr. Harding chuckled. He was a wiry guy with an impressive combover. "There's always a silver lining in every problem in life. But we're sure glad your dad's surgery went well."

"Thank you," Malcom said. "I'm very relieved. It will make traveling less stressful too."

"Of course." Mr. Harding picked up his water glass. "Lori sent us pictures and kept us updated on the renovation work you're doing at our house. It's all very impressive, so thank you."

Malcom shrugged as he took another helping of mashed potatoes. He couldn't seem to get enough of them. "I appreciate the place to stay. With the building project back on the docket, it's nice to have somewhere else to go home to that's not the same place I'm working at."

"That would be difficult," Mrs. Harding mused. Then she turned her attention to Lori and started asking about the shop.

Her questions were certainly persistent, and she seemed interested in every little detail. But Malcom decided he liked Lori's parents. They were comfortable together, and they seemed genuinely affectionate toward each other, giving one another the respect and space to talk. They teased each other and laughed together. It was interesting to watch a couple who'd been married for decades. He wondered what it would be like to be around his newly-reunited parents.

There was a time when they'd hardly speak to each other, but over the years, they seemed to have created a peace treaty and were at least civil. But now . . . had stranger things ever happened in any other family?

Malcom and Lori insisted they were on cleanup duty, although her parents still stuck around and helped. Malcom only excused himself when his mom called.

"Oh, thank goodness you're coming," she said through the phone. "We can finally be a family again. I don't like you and Bronson fighting."

Malcom was trying to catch up to her change of topic from his dad's life-threatening condition when she said, "Oh, and Bronson told me you're bringing a woman. I didn't know you had a girlfriend. Who is this person?"

"Mom," he said. "How's Dad?"

"He's sleeping, again." She sighed. "I don't know why he had to do this right before Thanksgiving. The hospital cafeteria isn't all that good, and all the food I bought for dinner is sitting at home."

Malcom would have laughed if they weren't talking about his dad's emergency surgery. "Well, there's always next Thanksgiving to make a turkey. Maybe a neighbor will take it off your hands."

"Turkey?" his mom said. "I didn't *buy* a turkey to bake. I ordered a to-go turkey dinner that was delivered to our house. All we have to do is warm it up. I was really looking forward to trying it out."

Malcom really had no response to that. Maybe worrying over an uneaten dinner was his mom's coping mechanism for extreme stress? "I'm sure the hospital will serve a special

Thanksgiving meal. Otherwise, it will be great to see you and Dad."

"Yes, yes," his mom said. "What time do you arrive?"

Malcom gave her the time.

"We'll see you then. I just hope this Lori woman is worth it. I don't understand why you and Penny didn't work out. I had a wonderful talk with her about an hour ago."

His mom had talked to *Penny*? *Why*?

She hung up before Malcom could ask her why in the world she would think that he'd ever want to date Penny. What had Bronson been telling his mom? Maybe Malcom didn't want to know, but it sure chased away any of the progress he'd felt he and Bronson had made in the last several hours.

Malcom pocketed his phone and returned to helping clean up the kitchen. Lori asked him if everything was okay, and he didn't offer much up. He didn't want to drag her into his new worries.

Once the kitchen was tidied and the food stored away, they all congregated at the kitchen table again with a bunch of board games. Malcom quickly learned that everyone in the Harding family was very competitive, and he really stood no chance. Luck gave him a couple of wins, but the overall winner was Mrs. Harding, who had no trouble gloating over the fact.

When Lori's parents finally went to bed, she hugged them both good night. It was kind of sweet.

"Don't stay up too late," Mr. Harding said, laying a hand on his shoulder and squeezing quite firmly.

"No, sir, we won't."

After her parents headed upstairs for the night, Lori turned to him. "You called my dad *sir*?"

"It seemed only fitting when he had my shoulder in a death grip."

Lori laughed. "He did not."

"Want to see the bruise?" He tugged at his collar.

"Stop." She stood from her chair and grabbed his hand to tug him upward. "Come on, let's watch TV or something on the couch. I'm tired, but not ready to abandon you yet."

Malcom walked with her willingly into the next room. "What's the *something*?"

A line appeared between her brows.

"You said let's watch TV or *something*."

"We're in my parents' house," she said pointedly.

He sat next to her on the couch. "TV it is."

Somehow Malcom fell asleep on the couch. When he awakened to a completely dark room with no flickering television light, he had a pillow beneath his head and a blanket draped over him. Courtesy of Lori, he knew. He lay still for a moment, as all of the events of the day before filtered through his mind. He hoped his father was comfortable and sleeping in his hospital room. He hoped his mom was getting rest too. He didn't know if Bronson had brought Kari with him—he'd never said.

And now Malcom wondered if it was a good idea to bring Lori into the middle of what could be a lot of family drama. Judging by his mother's words last night, she could very well be the one stirring everything up. But then he wondered if it would hurt Lori's feelings to uninvite her. The plane ticket was already bought.

He moved off the couch, folded the blanket, and set it on top of the pillow, then went to find his assigned room. As he headed along the hallway, he paused when he saw a light beneath Lori's bedroom door. Was she sleeping with the light on? Did he know that about her?

Or was she awake? He tapped softly on the door, so if she was asleep, she hopefully wouldn't wake up.

No one answered, and there was no sound, so he

continued on his way. As he reached the end of the hall, he heard a door click open.

Turning, he saw Lori standing there in something that was probably PJs to her, but still looked festive. A T-shirt with purple turkeys printed all over, and matching lounge pants.

"Malcom? Did you finally wake up?"

He smiled and leaned against the wall. "Yeah. Thanks for the pillow. Probably saved my neck."

"How are you feeling?" Her eyes glimmered with concern in the dim light.

"I'm fine, I think," he said. "Not exactly looking forward to seeing Bronson . . . later today. But it will be good to visit my dad."

She nodded and threaded her hands together in front of her.

"So . . ." he started in a hesitant voice. "I didn't tell you this before because Thanksgiving dinner was great, and I didn't want to spoil it more than I already have. But my mom has some hangups as to why I'm not dating Penny. I didn't know until we talked on the phone, and I'm assuming it's stemming from whatever Bronson is telling her in the hospital. Justifying all of his tax evasion stuff."

Lori blinked. "You can set your mom straight. She'll believe you, Malcom. You're her son."

He nodded at that. Hopefully Lori was right. "I just don't know what frame of mind she'll be in when you meet her. And I don't know how Bronson will treat you. Kari might be with him too."

Lori folded her arms. "If you don't want me to go, I won't go. You need to do what's right for you and your family. Not worry about me."

Malcom's stomach sank. "That's not the issue. I just . . ." He crossed to her and ran his hands up her arms, then rested his hands on her shoulders. "I don't want you to feel like they're picking on you. I really don't know how they'll act toward you in person. My mom ... she doesn't really have a filter, which is fine when someone I care about isn't the brunt of her comments. She can say whatever she wants about me, but not you."

Lori held his gaze. "It's not right for her to criticize you, either. Maybe I should come if only to defend you."

He let a small smile escape. "You would fight for my honor?"

"I'd fight to the death," she teased. Then she inched closer and looped her arms around his neck. "You're a remarkable man, Malcom. And if anyone is lucky to have you, it's your mom. And your dad. And Bronson."

He gave a short nod. "Yeah, can you tell them that?"

"Anytime." She smiled and pulled him closer to kiss him. "I'll call them or text them, or fly out to tell them in person. Just give me the word."

He leaned his forehead against hers. "You're already helping, Lori. And knowing there are people in Everly Falls who trust me, who have my back, and are willing to invest in my dream—it's overwhelming to think about. I'm so grateful."

Lori's fingers traced along the back of his neck. "I'm grateful to you. All of Everly Falls is grateful." She kissed him again, lingering longer this time. "Let me know what you want me to do. Whatever you need."

He bit his lip, then rested his forehead against hers. "I think I need to do this on my own. See my parents and figure out what they are together now. Talk to my brother alone—just the two of us. Figure out what can be salvaged."

"Okay," Lori said softly. "Just know that if you need any kneecaps broken, I'm ready."

He chuckled.

Then he drew her tightly against him, just breathing her in. Not just her scent, but her goodness. He did have to do this on his own, but he wouldn't really be alone. Not when he had Lori.

# Twenty-Three

LORI CHECKED HER TEXTS AS she burrowed inside her covers, with Tiger sitting on her chest, purring like a lawnmower. The group chat had finally quieted as everyone was probably going to sleep. And Malcom's last text had come in over an hour ago, after his plane landed. He should be back to Everly Falls by now.

He said he'd call her when he got home, but so far, nothing.

His father would remain in the hospital another day or two, but he was doing really well overall. He'd have a new health and nutrition regimen he was supposed to stick to. Malcom had told Lori it was strange to be around his parents—who so clearly doted on each other—after all this time.

She scrolled through the texts, skim reading a few of them again.

*And Bronson . . . Kari didn't come with him, which gave us a lot of time to talk. Without too much defensiveness.*

*Bronson wants to do a plea deal for tax evasion. The fines will be hefty, but he'll likely stay out of jail.*

*Kari's fines will be less, as well as Penny's.*

*I'll be glad when I'm home.*
*I'm missing you like crazy, sweetheart.*

He'd called her sweetheart, and he'd called Everly Falls *home*.

A knock sounded on her door, and she nearly jumped out of her skin. Tiger lifted his head, and she carefully moved him off her. How had she not heard someone on her stairs? And hadn't she locked the door at the bottom of the staircase?

A text buzzed her phone. From Malcom.

*I'm at your place.*

Relief flooded through her, and she headed to the door and opened it.

Malcom stood on the other side, a bouquet of flowers in hand. "Hey, I saw the light on."

She smiled. "Aren't you dead on your feet?"

"Never too dead for you."

She rolled her eyes, but then suddenly he was inside, pulling her into his arms. Squeezing her tight.

"I missed you," he murmured against her ear.

"I missed you too," she said. And it was true. Her heart was thumping, her feet at least an inch off the ground, and he smelled like he'd just stepped out of a shower. "I thought you were going to call me."

Malcom drew back, a half smile on his face, his hazel eyes warm. "I thought this would be better."

"I must say that I agree."

"Good." He leaned down and kissed her.

She nudged the door shut with her foot and kissed him back. His kiss was confident, familiar, and everything good that she'd memorized about him. How had she missed him so much after only a couple of days? His arms holding her, his hands splayed across her back, his seeking kisses—all of it made the butterflies rejoice in her stomach.

When she finally decided she should probably breathe a little, she drew away. "It's way too late for the grocery store to be open. Where did you get these flowers?"

He held them up. "I bought them in Montana. So they might need some water."

"Oh." Lori was surprised, but thrilled all the same. He'd carried flowers onto the plane? It kind of made her giddy. She stepped away from him and rummaged in her kitchen to find a vase. She couldn't remember the last time she'd put flowers in a vase—at least in winter.

Once she had the flowers situated, she turned toward Malcom. He looked deliciously rumpled after their kiss. She needed something to distract herself. "Are you hungry? Thirsty? I can warm up pasta I made earlier tonight. Or . . ."

"I'm fine."

Tiger interrupted with a meow.

Malcom bent to pick up the kitten. True to his nature, Tiger began to purr. "He missed me too."

"I'm making you something. Airplane food doesn't cut it." Lori moved about the kitchen, warming up the chicken and pasta. She cut up some fruit and made an impromptu fruit salad. "Nothing like my mom's extravagant Thanksgiving meal, but here you go."

"Lori, you really didn't have to do this." But he sat down and began to eat anyway.

For some reason, it brought her immense satisfaction to be taking care of him this way. Not that he couldn't do it himself, but she wanted to serve him. Feed him. Nourish him. She sat next to him, and he linked her fingers with his free hand.

"Don't feed the cat," Lori warned when Tiger meowed like he was starving.

Malcom paused. "You're telling me you ate this same meal for dinner but didn't give him one piece of chicken?"

"I didn't. I gave him two pieces."

Malcom laughed. When he finished eating, he tugged her chair closer. "I promise I didn't come over here to get you to feed me."

"Oh, don't worry," she said. "I don't think that. I mean, I'm a passable cook, but nothing that would motivate a person to drive over so late at night."

"Mm-hmm." He lifted his hand and brushed his thumb along her jaw. "What's with the Christmas PJs?"

Lori glanced down at her person. Yes, it was true, she was wearing one of her pairs of Christmas PJs—this particular set had multicolored Christmas trees on them. "Well, Thanksgiving is over."

"It's not even December yet."

She gave him her sternest look. "Christmas is in twenty-eight days. It's practically over."

Malcom laughed, then he tugged her onto his lap. Just as she grasped his shoulders for balance, he nuzzled her neck.

Lori decided she liked Malcom late at night in her apartment. His presence filled the space with everything delicious.

"So, what are you doing tomorrow, sweetheart?" he murmured against her skin.

His endearment sent warm goose bumps across her skin. "Do you even have to ask that? Decorating for Christmas."

He lifted his head. "The store? I thought I saw the window decorated when I pulled up."

"Oh, the store is already finished," she said. "I've got to decorate my apartment, and if I have time left over, your place. Which is technically my parents' place."

His smile appeared. "Wait, is that part of the rental agreement?"

She stroked her fingers through his hair. "There isn't a

rental agreement, so I can do whatever I want as the landlord. Don't be surprised if there's a Christmas tree in the living room when you get home."

"Hmm." He kissed the edge of her jaw. "I'll see what I can do to help. Right after I check on the condo project."

"Yeah, right after you save the world, or more specifically, Everly Falls."

He drew back with a wince. "Don't let my mom hear you say that. She's still holding out hope for Bronson and me to start a new company together, and for me to date Penny."

He'd said some of this on the phone, but hearing it in person made Lori realize that Malcom's issues with his family were still battering him.

"Invite your parents out here," she said on a complete impulse. She heard herself say the words, but couldn't quite believe it.

Malcom stared at her. "You want them to come here?"

"Yeah," Lori said, her impulsiveness growing more confident. "You can show them around the job site, and they can meet your friends."

"What about my girlfriend?"

"They should definitely meet her. I mean, if we're really calling ourselves boyfriend- girlfriend, which you constantly do, then I might as well meet them sooner than later. Not that I think I'm going to charm your parents on a first meeting, but at least it will give them a face to talk about behind my back."

Malcom smirked, running his fingers along her jaw. He leaned in and kissed her, softly. "I'd love for my parents to meet you, but only if you really want to. You told me your shop has a full Christmas schedule."

"It does," Lori said with a shrug. "But I have Marci, and we talked about hiring a couple of teenagers for afternoons and evenings. So whatever works for your parents, I can swing it. When your dad can travel, of course."

Malcom's gaze didn't leave her face, his smile appearing. "You're definitely my girlfriend, then. I'm not bringing my parents out here with us being just friends."

"Does this feel like just friends?" she asked, pressing her mouth at the edge of his. "Or this?" She kissed the other side of his mouth.

"No," Malcom said in a rasp, his hold tightening. "It feels like I'm the only man you're ever going to look at again."

Lori laughed, then kissed him straight on the mouth.

By the next day, after spilling the beans to her friend group, and Malcom making a phone call to his parents, Lori was wondering what she'd gotten herself into.

Yeah, she still felt it was a good thing to officially meet Malcom's parents. Her growing relationship with him would benefit, and hopefully it would get his mom to stop daydreaming of that woman Penny. Yet . . . what was that saying? Be careful what you wish for?

Because they were now planning to come to Everly Falls in two weeks. Right in the middle of the holiday season. At least it would give her time to prepare . . . as well as plenty of time to worry about every little thing.

Her phone buzzed with a new round of texts as she sat in her parents' old kitchen. The place had new counters and new flooring now.

*Is this a record for you, Lori?* Brandy wrote. *Have you ever met the parents of a man you've been dating?*

*Not that I can remember, and there aren't a lot of men to remember,* she wrote.

*He is so in to you,* Stephenie texted. *I mean, he does whatever you ask him to.*

*Golden retriever,* Julie added. *I should know. I married one.*

Laughing emojis were exchanged.

*Well, he needs to tone that down,* Lori wrote, half-serious. *I made him dinner last night, and you would have thought he'd glimpsed heaven.*

*Wait! He came over last night?* Brandy texted. *Details and pics if you have them.*

*There are no pics! I need to get back to decorating now.* Lori left them all hanging. She shouldn't have said anything because she didn't want her friends to get the wrong idea. But what would the wrong idea be? That she liked Malcom more and more each day? That every moment with him seemed better than the last?

She was really, truly, in a relationship, and it was hard to wrap her mind around it sometimes.

Lori headed into the living room of her parents' house. She'd already set up the artificial tree, and now all she had to do was decorate it. Digging through the boxes she'd hauled from the attic, she found herself wading through memory lane. Apparently her parents had never thrown away one Christmas craft or decoration. When they'd moved, they'd sold stuff she didn't want or they hadn't wanted to take with them.

But they'd left the boxes of seasonal decorations in the attic, with Lori intending on taking them to the store one day and sorting them. That day had come. Going through each box, she thought back to her childhood memories. She really had grown up in a great family, and she had always been grateful—but even more so lately.

She wanted that for Malcom too—some peace in his family. She hoped that when his parents came, he'd find that. And if they didn't like her right away, that was okay. There was time. And Lori didn't mind the wait. She realized, for the first time, that everything to do with Malcom would be worth the wait.

Their relationship had felt both fast and slow. But mostly,

it felt natural. Like things were progressing how they should. Malcom was respectful of her time, and he always asked her opinions. He didn't shy away from telling her his own thoughts, and sharing his own desires.

Which made him a gem of a person.

Mostly, Lori realized, of all the things she felt grateful for—in the here and now—she was grateful for Malcom.

The rumble of a truck outside pulled her from her thoughts. Lori climbed to her feet and parted the drapes to look. It was Malcom's truck, and it wasn't even sunset. Had he finished early today? Or was there some problem at the job site?

He surely knew she was here because her car was parked at the curb.

She reached the door and opened it just as he stepped onto the porch. A memory—no, a future possibility—rolled through her mind. What would it be like to share a home together? To greet Malcom each night after both of their jobs were finished for the day? To share their meals together. To unwind and talk about their day? To not have to say goodbye to each other at night?

Was that what she wanted? With *this* man?

Her heart whispered *yes,* and her brain agreed.

## Twenty-Four

THERE WERE STILL TWO MORE weeks until Christmas, but Everly Falls was in the throes of the holiday. Each night, community events abounded, and tonight, there was a hot chocolate cook-off—or boil-off?—at Lori's shop. Restaurant chefs and bakery shop owners and regular home cooks had all entered the contest. Fifteen of them, Lori had said.

And Malcom was one of the judges. He enjoyed chocolate and sweets and hot chocolate, like most people. But to be a *judge*? He wasn't sure why he agreed to such a plan. Oh yeah. Because anything that Lori asked of him, his immediate response was *yes*.

Austin had given him a hard time about it the other day. But then again, he had rescheduled one of their appointments because of Everly.

Malcom supposed they were equally whipped over their women.

Which was why he hoped that this weekend would be smooth sailing with his parents in town. He pulled to a stop in front of the airport pickup lane. Up ahead, he could see a fifty-something blonde woman, wearing a bright yellow utility vest, waving people away from the curb. "No waiting. Drive around again," he heard her say.

He could drive around again, but he was pretty sure his parents would be appearing at any moment.

And he didn't want to make his dad stand too long or wait in the cold. It had just started to rain—lightly, but it was an icy rain with the temperature to nearly freezing.

The yellow vest drew closer. Three cars away. Now two cars.

His phone rang. "Hi, Mom."

"We're out of the airport," she said breathlessly. "Where are you parked? Oh, there you are."

Just as she said it, he saw his parents. Together. It was a strange sight to see.

A knock on his window made him jump.

"I'll pull closer," he told his mom, then hung up. He opened his window. "My parents are right there."

The woman peered to where he pointed. "All right, have a good evening, sir."

He planned on it. Opening his door, he climbed out to greet his parents, then loaded their luggage into one side of the rear seat. His dad looked so much healthier than he had in the hospital, but it was also clear that he'd lost weight. His mom was her usually bustling self, with a fresh short haircut, heeled boots, and silver hoop earrings. She insisted that his dad sit up front, and she fussed over him until his seat belt was secure and he'd located his cell phone.

"Dad's calling Bronson on our way into your little town," Mom said. "He said he wanted to know our schedule."

Malcom tried not to let his irritation show. Tonight and the next couple of days would be about his parents getting to know Lori. He didn't want Bronson in the mix, or even to be a concern for his parents. At the end of the weekend, he'd be taking them to his brother's house, where they planned to stay for a few more days. Bronson would have plenty of time with them.

But Malcom didn't protest. He turned on his blinker and pulled out of the pickup lane, then merged into traffic.

"It's colder than I thought it would be here," Mom said. Colder than Montana?

"It rains a lot in December," Malcom said. "Better than snow, maybe?"

"It's not Christmas without snow," she said, her voice taking on a whiny edge. "You should reconsider your holiday plans. We should all be together as a family. Bronson is coming with Kari up to Montana, you know."

He knew. And it could very well be Christmas without snow. The original Christmas didn't have snow, so why was that so important? Plus, there was no way Lori could get more than Christmas Day off from her shop. Holidays were busy for retail owners, and he wasn't about to ditch her.

His dad began to speak into his phone to Bronson. "It's a chili cook-off," Dad said. "Nothing I can eat, so I don't know what I'm having for dinner."

"It's a *hot chocolate* contest," Malcom said, loud enough that surely Bronson could hear. "And Lori already has dinner for us at the place I'm staying. It won't be chili, Dad."

"He says it's not chili. But I can't have hot chocolate either."

"You don't have to have the hot chocolate, dear," Mom said from the back seat, resting a hand on his shoulder.

"Ice skating," Dad said. "I can't do that either. I guess I'll sit and watch while I freeze."

"We'll have coats, and we're watching a *performance indoors*, Dad. We're not ice skating ourselves," Malcom corrected.

"Here, let me talk to him," his mom said, holding out her hand for the phone.

He handed it over. While his mom began to speak to

Bronson, who apparently was getting filled in on every minute of their schedule in detail, Dad said, "Mom told me we were ice skating."

"No," Malcom said. He turned on the headlights as the sun sank behind the horizon, turning the sky violet. "We're only doing things that you can do with us. We're not leaving you behind. Maybe next year we can ice skate if you want."

His dad seemed thoughtful, despite the one-sided conversation in the back seat. "Okay, maybe I'll do it. I haven't ice skated for years."

Malcom didn't remember any time that his father had ice skated.

"Oh my goodness," his mother said, her voice elevated with excitement. "That's wonderful news! How far along is she?" A pause. "Oh, that's too bad she's feeling sick. Do you need us to cut our trip short in Everly Falls and come help you out?"

What in the world was she talking about?

He found out soon enough.

"Kari's pregnant," his mom announced as soon as she hung up with Bronson. "Two months along. She's been really sick this week."

She squeezed Dad's shoulder. "We're going to be grandparents."

Dad reached up and clasped their hand.

Malcom was happy for Bronson and Kari—maybe starting a family would keep them making better choices for their future. But he was a bit puzzled about his mom's reaction. Bronson wasn't her son, but apparently, she was one hundred percent into Dad's life. Which was how it should have been, in the beginning, without all the detours.

As they turned off the highway and took the exit to Everly Falls, his mom screeched, "Oh my goodness!"

Malcom almost slammed on the brakes. "What? What is it?"

"I need to call Penny right now," she said.

Malcom couldn't think of a worse sentence coming from her mouth. "What's going on, Mom? What's happening with Penny?"

"Shh."

Did his mom really shush him?

"Penny!" she said into her phone. "I just saw the Facebook post! Congratulations!"

Malcom frowned. His mother was on Facebook? Since when?

Penny was talking, but all he could hear was his mom's responses. She didn't hang up until they were almost to Lori's parents' old house.

"Well, that's that," she said. "You missed your chance with Penny. Her ex-husband wants to reunite, and they got engaged today. It's a done deal."

Why would Malcom care about Penny becoming engaged to another man? "Good for her."

"What do you mean *good for her*?" Mom snapped. "You broke her heart. You threw away a perfectly good thing. Just think, you and Bronson married to sisters. It would have been amazing."

"No, Mom." Malcom slowed his truck and stopped in front of a closed shoe store.

"Is this it?" his dad said. "It's awfully dark."

"No, the house is one street over," he said. "We need to talk before I take you to meet my girlfriend."

"You shouldn't use the word *girlfriend* so lightly," Mom said. "This Lori woman might get ideas."

Malcom exhaled, frustration rolling through him. "Look, I need both of you to listen to me. Lori *is* my girlfriend, and

I'm not saying that lightly. I love her. I'm in love with her. She's it for me. She might not know it yet, but it's true."

In the dimness of the truck's cab, both of his parents' gazes were locked on him.

"That means, I don't want you to bring up Penny at all when you're around Lori," he said. "We've already been through enough distress with Penny—who by the way, was never the right woman for me. I never wanted to date her, even before the company fiasco. I was *never* interested in her as more than a coworker, not even a little bit."

Neither of his parents said anything for a moment.

Then his father spoke. "You truly love this Lori woman?"

"I do." He released a slow breath. "I haven't exactly told her yet, so please don't spill the beans. We're taking things slowly."

His mother's lips had pursed, and he could only guess her opinion. Which was ridiculous that she'd *have* an opinion—she hadn't even met Lori.

Malcom pulled out onto the neighborhood street, then drove the couple of blocks to where the house was. The lights were on, and it seemed that Lori had added more Christmas lights to the bushes out front. Malcom had to smile at that. "By the way," he said, "Lori loves holidays—it's kind of her thing."

"Is that why she opened a holiday shop?" Dad asked.

"Yep."

Mom still hadn't said anything, and Malcom decided that her attitude was on her.

He parked and turned off the engine, then he unloaded their luggage. They'd stay at the house on the bed he'd bought. He'd use an air mattress in the second bedroom. Before he reached the front door, he could already smell the dinner Lori had made. He'd told her to not go to too much trouble, to order something from the deli. But when he opened the door, he could see the kitchen table spread with a feast.

Lori came out of the kitchen, wiping her hands on a Christmas-themed hand towel. Her face was flushed, which told him she had gone to a lot of trouble. Her green long-sleeved shirt said *Naughty or Nice*, and her earrings were dangling red ornaments. Her hair was down, but held back by a headband decorated with mistletoe. Classic Lori.

"Hello," she said with a smile that Malcom could tell was nervous.

He quickly introduced everyone, and he was happy his mom said, "It's great to finally meet you," in a voice that sounded perfectly pleasant.

Who cared if she was more quiet than usual—that might be a good thing, right?

Dad asked Lori a bunch of questions as they gathered around the table, and she cheerfully answered.

"I didn't know what you like to eat," she said as they all sat down. "I looked up heart-healthy dishes, so you can eat everything here without worry, Mr. Graves. But I made plenty extra, so you can have leftovers throughout your stay if you want to relax after some of our activities."

Malcom saw his mom's appraising gaze as she set a napkin in her lap. She didn't crack a smile though, keeping her expression impassive.

It was quite amusing, really, to see how much of a chatterbox his dad became when his mom went sullen.

Dad asked all kinds of questions about the shop, and Lori happily answered them. "Oh, I almost forgot." She rose from the table and fetched a small, wrapped box from the counter. "This is for you," she told Malcom's mom.

Mom looked like she was about to swallow her tongue as she took the box. "Oh? What's this about?"

"Just a small welcoming gift," Lori said. "It reminded me of you."

Mom's eyes narrowed, but she continued removing the wrapping. She revealed a jewelry box, then opened it. Inside was a set of turquoise jewelry.

"It's beautiful," she said, lifting her gaze. "I wasn't expecting a gift."

Lori shrugged. "Malcom told me you love turquoise jewelry, and I saw this in one of my vendors' catalogs. It's all custom, so I kind of took a shot in the dark of what to have designed for you."

Mom lifted out the necklace, then the earrings. "This is a custom design?" Lori nodded. "It's lovely." She examined it for a few moments. "I don't know what to say. It's beautiful."

Lori only smiled, and Malcom reached for her hand and squeezed it.

"We should head over to the shop soon," she said. "If you'd like to be a judge, Mr. Graves, I'm sure they could use another one. Malcom has already been roped in."

Dad chuckled. "I would if I didn't have to watch my sugar intake."

"Fair enough," Lori said. "Why don't the two of you get settled into the bedroom, and Malcom and I will clean up the meal."

# Twenty-Five

ONCE HIS PARENTS DISAPPEARED DOWN the hall, Malcom drew Lori into his arms. "You're amazing, do you know that?"

Lori lifted her chin and met his hazel eyes. She brushed a finger across his jaw, enjoying the bristles. "I like your parents. And your mom's bite is more like a nip."

"She's hardly spoken a word," he said.

"She doesn't need to. I'm pretty sure I know what she wants to say."

"Is that why you bought her a gift?"

Lori smiled. "I saw it and knew it would be perfect for her." She lifted a shoulder, then slipped her arms about his neck. "But a little appreciation always goes a long way."

"Mm-hmm." Malcom bent to kiss her.

She wished they could enjoy kissing a little more. But his parents were only steps away.

"Come on, let's get to work," she said, with a playful push to his chest. In a short time, she and Malcom had the leftovers packed away and the table cleared.

"Oh, by the way," he said, snagging her hand as they crossed paths. "Bronson's wife is two months pregnant, and Penny's engaged to one of her exes. Not sure which one."

Lori stared at him. "Wow. Those are both big things."

"Yeah, really big." Malcom ran a thumb over her fingers, which were still intertwined with his. "And it's good news for me, for us. Maybe Bronson will finally take more responsibility in life, and well, good riddance to Penny."

Lori smirked. "Are you going to miss being the obsession of another woman?"

He shook his head. "I don't mind being *your* obsession."

She lifted her brows. "You'll never be able to prove it." She might be playing hardball with him, but she pressed a kiss on his mouth, so maybe not at all.

"I need to tell you one more thing, though."

"You're making my head spin, Mr. Graves."

He ran his free hand along her neck, then rested it on her shoulder. "I hope it's in a good way, but I told my parents something. And I should have told you first."

Lori waited, expectant.

He drew in a steadying breath and scanned her face. "I told them that I'm in love with you."

*Had he really said* . . . Lori didn't move, didn't speak.

"I've known it for a while," he continued in a low rumble. "Maybe when you offered to go with me to Montana to see my father. Or maybe when you agreed to be my fake date."

"We'd barely met back then," she said in a quiet voice. She blinked at the sudden moisture in her eyes.

"I can't exactly define the moment, but it's here." He drew her hand to his chest, right over his heart, and she could feel it thumping. "You're in my heart. And every time I'm with you, it's like my entire being is filled up. I love you, sweetheart, and I hope that doesn't scare you away."

A tear fell onto her cheek, and she swiped it away. Where had this man come from and how had he ended up in her life? She marveled at everything he was. "Look up, Malcom."

Confusion creased his brow, but he looked up. Above them dangled some mistletoe. In fact, there were multiple bunches of mistletoe hanging from the ceiling, continuing into the living room. "What have you done?" he asked with a laugh, although it sounded like his heart was in his throat.

"I've strategically placed mistletoe throughout the house so there will be no shortage of kissing . . . you."

"Hmm," he murmured, his gaze back on her. "So I haven't scared you off? You're giving me a lot of hope, and I like all of your ideas."

Lori moved her fingers along the base of his neck, making goose bumps spread across his skin.

"I kind of wish my parents would leave now," he whispered. "I'd rather have you all to myself. After the hot chocolate event, of course."

"They can't leave until I win them over," she said, her tone mostly serious.

"I told you their opinion doesn't matter to me," he said. "They already know how I feel about you, and they'll have to get used to it."

She melted a little at his words and anchored her arms about his neck. She should tell him. He deserved to know. "It's important to me, Malcom, because I love you too."

He stared at her for a moment. His eyes focused on her, steady and true. "Really?" he whispered.

"Really."

He drew her flush against him, lifting her off the ground as he kissed her. She was definitely melting now. Deep down, she'd never feel so connected to any other person besides him.

They only broke apart because of the sounds of his parents' footsteps from the hallway.

Lori straightened her mistletoe headband. Surely, her cheeks were Christmas red when she turned to face Malcom's parents.

His mom's smile seemed genuine though, and she wore the turquoise jewelry set.

"That looks lovely on you," Lori told her.

She beamed. "Thank you so much. I really appreciate the gift."

Malcom moved his hand along Lori's back. "Everyone ready?" he asked.

"Let's go," his mom said.

Lori crossed to his dad and linked arms. "I need to warn you, your son's kind of a big deal around here. People will want to ask you all kinds of questions."

"Oh?" Mr. Graves said. "I think I could manage that."

They filed out of the house, and as Malcom shut and locked the front door, his mom paused with him on the porch. "I like her," she said simply.

Lori wasn't sure if she was meant to overhear, but she felt a bubble of giddiness move through her.

"She has a generous heart," Malcom's mom continued. "And I'm not talking about the gift. You're different around her. There's a light in your eyes when you look at her—something I've never seen with anyone else."

Lori knew his dad was listening too, because he squeezed her arm.

"I should have put more trust in your decisions all along," Mrs. Graves added. "Thanks for being patient with me."

Lori guessed it was probably the most sincere and real thing Malcom had ever heard his mom say. As for Lori, her heart had just expanded three times. Yeah, things in Malcom's family were definitely complicated. But maybe it was possible for everyone to move past all the betrayals and find a new sense of peace.

By the time Malcom joined them at the truck, Lori was settled in the front seat. "They insisted," she said with a laugh. "And your parents can be pretty persistent."

He only smiled and reached for her hand, then proceeded to back the truck out of the driveway with one hand. Easy.

When they parked at the store, it was already bustling with setup. Marci was there, directing everyone to their places.

Malcom introduced his parents to those he knew, and Lori took over the rest. During the next couple of hours, all of her friends showed up, and she observed his parents chatting to plenty of townspeople. She had situated them at one of the tables with some padded chairs, next to a space heater. With the shop door opening and closing so much, the temperature remained brisk.

Each time his mom laughed, Lori smiled to herself, her confidence growing. They'd won over the woman. Who knew it would be as simple as bringing her to Everly Falls? Right now, she was chatting with Lydia, who'd done a full one-eighty in her opinion of the condo project—which now seemed to be paying off big—and Malcom.

Apparently finished with his judging of the hot chocolate, Malcom now chatted easily with the townspeople as well, although mostly Austin and Cal, who'd come with Everly and Brandy. All the guys were good-looking in their own way, but there was something special about Malcom. *Her* man. She liked the sound of that. And he'd told her he loved her. Another round of giddy bubbles floated through her. He'd told his *parents,* and then he'd told her. Was it possible to feel so happy, so content?

She loved that he'd made solid friends, and she loved that he'd put his heart and soul into the condo project—making things right.

"Hey," Lori said, sliding her hand into his. He turned to look at her, linking their fingers as he smiled. She had the urge to kiss him, right then and there, in front of half the town. "Looks like your parents are enjoying themselves."

Malcom drew her closer. "They are. I don't think I've seen my parents enjoy an event together this much. Of course, I haven't seen them together much since I was a kid."

He released her hand and draped an arm about her shoulders. She leaned into him and wrapped her arm around his waist. "I'm glad they're having fun." She tilted her head up to find him gazing at her.

"Is there some mistletoe in the hallway over there?"

She glanced where he'd indicated. The hallway split off to the storage room, and beyond was the door that led to her apartment. "I don't think so."

"What?" He touched one of her ornament earrings, making it bob. "You have mistletoe all over the house, even on your headband, yet you only have . . ." He craned his neck to look around. "One sprig by the front door."

Lori bit her lip and considered. "You're right. We definitely need more mistletoe in the shop."

"Where do you keep it?" he asked.

She gazed at him with surprise. He was really getting into this Christmas decorating thing. "There's a box in the storage room."

Malcom steered her away from the main shop, toward the storage room.

"What's gotten into you?" she asked with a laugh.

He kissed her on the cheek. "You."

She laughed again and opened the storage room. After turning on the light, it didn't take long to find the box. Malcom pulled out only one sprig, then cut off a piece of twine from the giant roll on a shelf. Then he grabbed her hand and led her out of the room, turning off the light. This left the hallway dim, and he reached up and found a place to hang the sprig of mistletoe, securing it tightly with the twine.

"There," he said. "Much better."

"You're totally hooked on Christmas, aren't you?"

"That's one way to put it." He settled his hands at her waist, and she reciprocated by resting her hands on his biceps.

Leaning close, he whispered in her ear, "Did I tell you that I like your earrings?"

She smiled, her skin pebbling. "I don't remember. You'll have to tell me again." She felt his smile against her neck.

"I like your earrings," he whispered. "But I love you."

She laughed. "And I love you."

He kissed her, like she expected, but she didn't expect the surge of emotion that swelled inside of her. Every day—no, every moment—seemed to get better with Malcom. She slid her hands up his arms and settled them behind his neck, drawing him closer and kissing him back. His mouth was soft, warm, seeking, as if telling her they had all the time in the world. Because he wasn't going anywhere, and neither was she.

It had definitely been a good call to hang more mistletoe.

Want to read Brandy and Ian's story?
Read the first two chapters of JUST ADD MISCHIEF here:

# One

PEOPLE.

Ian Hudson could hear *people*.

Duke barked, and Ian snapped, "Hush, boy."

Not that he was opposed to people in general, but he'd bought acres of this hillside in order to have peace and quiet. When he wanted to hear other people, he could drive into Everly Falls, grab a meal, get a haircut, buy some groceries. But when he was home and working on his newfound hobby, he didn't want to be disturbed by chatter or the sound of cars passing by or a lawn mower.

A woman's laugh bounced against the walls of his woodworking shed. Well, it was a full-blown workshop, with state-of-the-art machinery. Something he'd invested in a year ago when everything in his life had upended. Ironically, he was fine with the sounds *he* made, whether he was constructing a piece of furniture or repairing something.

Duke pressed his nose against the low window of the workshop, as if he could see through the sawdust film on the glass. He whined, hoping for what would not happen. There was no way Ian was letting the golden retriever out of the workshop, because he'd just bound toward the people and act like he had a set of new best friends.

How close were the people outside? There wasn't another house or cabin for a couple of miles, unless one counted the old Miller place. It was more of a cottage near the main road—which was the only paved road around. The Miller cottage hadn't been available for purchase, since the county owned the property that ran parallel to the rural highway. Ian had inquired.

Maybe they were hikers, and they'd pass by in a couple minutes. He should just return to his work. Instead, he pulled off his safety goggles. "Stay here, Duke, and no barking," he commanded the dog, despite his soulful brown eyes begging to come along.

Ian strode out of the workshop. A quick glance around didn't show the hikers—but he could still hear their voices. Two women, it sounded like. Then a lower rumble followed. A man was with them, too.

Curious, Ian strode along the path that connected to the narrow dirt road that led to his cabin in one direction, then to the main road in the other direction, right past the old Miller place. Perhaps the hikers had already finished their excursion and had come across the quaint cottage. It needed a lot of work to ever be inhabitable, but any passerby could see the charm of the place.

Ian wasn't planning on speaking to the hikers or introducing himself. He just wanted to make sure they weren't going to snoop around. Or heaven forbid, trespass on his own property. Through the trees, he spotted a wide swath of color that had to be a car. Red, to be exact. And another color. White. Belonging to a truck.

The voices were louder now, cheerful, and there was a lot of walking back and forth.

Ian's gut twisted. *No*... The next few steps brought three people into clearer view—two women and a man. And they were... moving stuff into the cottage.

They couldn't be squatters. Their vehicles and clothing and furniture negated that idea. Then who were these people, and what gave them the right to move into an abandoned cottage? Surely, nothing in that place worked—was the water and sewer even hooked up? Not to mention the electricity.

Ian set his hands on his hips, debating whether to call the county offices, or to confront the trio himself. It was Saturday, so it might be hard to get the county office to answer the phone—unless he called the emergency number. Which was probably reserved for forest fires. And this wasn't exactly an emergency...

With a heavy sigh, Ian cut through the trees, taking the shortcut path to the cottage. He knew his approach wouldn't be silent—there were too many fallen autumn leaves that crunched under his boots. When he emerged, he found three people staring at him.

"Oh, you scared me," one of the women said. Her sandy-blonde hair was tied up in a peach-colored scarf, and her shirt was a kaleidoscope of colors he probably couldn't name.

The other woman stood on the porch, shaded by the roof. She held a box on her hip and didn't seem all that startled. Her gaze was curious, and she took her time scanning him from head to foot.

He probably had sawdust in his hair, and his work jeans were not much cleaner. He was pretty sure the T-shirt beneath his flannel shirt had wood stain on it—no amount of laundry detergent could ever get it out. Not that he cared about the state of his clothing and hair, but he knew plenty of people in Everly Falls were quick to judge—small town and all.

Maybe he should have moved to a big city—he'd be more

anonymous—because by the looks of it, his carefully arranged tranquility and peace had come to an end.

The man stepped forward. Dark hair, dark eyes, around six two, which set him a couple of inches shorter than Ian. "You the neighbor up the road?" the man asked.

His expression was friendly, open, and that annoyed Ian. He wasn't interested in chitchat or making friends.

"Neighbor?" Ian rasped. "To whom?"

The man swept a hand toward the woman on the porch. She was still standing in the shade of the roof, but he could see that she was blonde, pretty in a high-maintenance way, and petite enough that she'd probably blow away in the next storm coming through the hills.

"Brandy's moving in today," the man continued. "We heard there was a resident up here."

"You mean a recluse," the woman with the peach scarf said with a laugh. She turned her smiling hazel eyes on Ian. "You look normal enough, though."

He must not be doing his best glower, so he folded his arms. "And you all are . . . ?"

"I'm Austin Hayes, and this is my fiancé, Everly Kane."

Ian's frown deepened. "Everly, as in Everly Falls?"

The peach-scarf woman waved away his question. "Yeah, sure. It's old news. This is my sister, Brandy. Seems like you've got a new neighbor."

Brandy still hadn't spoken, but her eyes remained locked on him.

"You're Ian Hudson, right? The retired financier?" Everly continued. "Don't see you in town much."

"Don't go to town much," he deadpanned, keeping his arms folded. "I thought this was county property. Are you, uh, employed by the county? Are they renting to you or something?"

*Please say yes, and please say that no one is actually moving into the cottage, and I won't have any neighbors.*

"Nope," Everly said. "My sister is moving in. She went through a recent, uh, life event and other things, and my mom begged her to stay in Everly Falls, and this was a compromise."

Ian wasn't sure of all that Everly had said, but she hadn't answered+ his question.

"You're *not* renting? The county wouldn't sell to me—so why would they sell to you?" Maybe Ian was being rude, but he needed to know.

"Here's the thing," Everly said as Austin came to stand by her. The pair linked hands. "My great-grandad built this place, and when the county bought his property from him, the deed stated that his descendants could still live here until the county develops the land." She spread her arms. "Nothing's developed, so here we are."

Ian knew he was frowning, but this was all news to him. How did he not know about the deed? "I thought you said your last name was Kane."

"Miller is our mother's side," Everly clarified.

Ian rubbed the back of his neck. So. The waif of a woman standing on the porch, apparently mute, was moving into this dilapidated cottage. Maybe she was a quiet person? Unlike her chatty sister?

"I'm *so* glad you'll have such a close neighbor, Brandy," Everly said. "We could come up for barbecues and other neighborly activities." She grinned at Ian, then Austin. "What do you think, guys?"

"Sounds good to me," Austin said, his mouth quirked.

Both Brandy and Ian remained mute.

"I could use a hand if you've got a little time," Austin added, motioning toward the bed of the truck. Furniture pieces had been strapped in, and they would definitely be awkward for a person to carry single-handedly.

And that was how Ian ended up not only meeting his new neighbor, but also helping her move in.

# Two

"Where do you want this?" a low voice asked.

Brandy turned from where she'd just set down a box on the kitchen counter, which had seen better days.

Ian Hudson filled the entire doorway of the cottage, carrying a box marked "Kitchen."

Brandy tapped the counter. "Here is fine." She didn't have a lot of possessions, and they'd been more than halfway done when Ian had showed up. She'd cringed when Austin had asked for his help because the man's scowl seemed to be a permanent feature on his face.

When he'd strode out of the woods, she thought she'd gone back a few hundred years in time, and Paul Bunyan had just appeared. She'd heard about Ian Hudson, of course. Moved to Everly Falls last year sometime. Brandy had been planning her wedding to Brock Hayes and hadn't paid much attention to the town gossip. Now, she wished she could at least remember something.

She wondered how a financier—a geek, in other words—had the build of a pro-athlete. The breadth of his shoulders made him look like he could uproot one of the pine trees outside her cottage with his bare hands.

Brandy tried not to stare as Ian strode toward her now, his boots clomping on the bare hardwood floor, which needed a good sanding and probably new stain. Despite olive skin, his dark hair and dark glower, his eyes were a surprising light green. Right now, they were icy, and he seemed to have no problem returning her stare.

"Thanks," she said as the box thumped on the counter. "I think we're good from here. Appreciate your help, though."

Ian and Austin had carried in all the furniture already, and now Austin and Everly were outside, cutting back the overgrown bushes in front of the house. Brandy had told them it could all wait until next weekend, but Everly hadn't listened to her.

"You staying long?" Ian asked.

This close up, Brandy had to lift her chin to meet his gaze. How tall was he? At five seven, Brandy wasn't a shrimp, but this guy was really tall. And did she mention he was built? Like he didn't spend any of his time on the couch. No TV series bingeing for this man.

Not like Brock, her ex, who spent hours in the gym to bulk up. No, this man had a more natural build.

"What do you mean by *long*?" Brandy asked. No matter the size of this mountain man, she wasn't going to let his hard tone and direct questions bother her. She had no problem throwing questions back into his face. Who did he think he was anyway? She was legitimately here, and he could stay on his *own* property, and out of her way.

Brandy wasn't exactly familiar with this section of the hills. The waterfall hikes were several miles down the road, and she didn't know if she'd been up this way much since she was a kid, and they'd drive by "Grandpa's cottage" every so often.

Ian rested one of his large hands on the edge of the counter. "You don't look like the nature type. Maybe living in the woods is fun for a short vacation, but you're moving a lot of stuff into this cottage. Tells me you're staying longer than a week or two."

Brandy folded her arms. "*Nature type?* What do you mean by that?" Again, she was asking a question instead of answering *his* questions. She didn't know why she wanted to irk the man, except he'd irked her. Blasting out of those trees like he owned the place, suspicion in those clear green eyes of his. Not to mention his perpetual scowl and accusatory words.

"I mean . . ." His voice trailed off as he scanned her person, from the flip-flops she wore to her yellow capris and white-and-yellow blouse, to the strand of pearls at her neck. His gaze lingered, then lifted again to her face.

She felt a blush coming on, not because this man's perusal of her person was flattering, but because she was angry that he was judging her. He sounded like her mom. *Why would you want to live so far from civilization? You don't even know how to change a flat tire. What if the internet goes out? What if you get sick and can't drive into town to see the doctor?*

It wasn't that Brandy was helpless. She was a grown woman with a college accounting degree. She freelanced as a CPA, and she also worked for a nonprofit that funded wells in Africa. So she didn't need to be in an established office. Yes, she relied heavily on the internet, but she was going to get that figured out with the hot-spot subscription she'd added through her cell phone carrier. She'd been to *Africa* on humanitarian trips—places way more rural and primitive than Grandpa Miller's cottage.

Nature was just that—nature. Trees, leaves, dirt, and rocks.

"You just look more . . ." Ian paused. "Used to the city life."

Brandy was pretty sure he was going to say something else. What exactly, she didn't know, but she could see the contempt, or was it suspicion, in his eyes.

"I love the hills," she said. "I love trees. I love fresh air. And I'm looking forward to a lot of quiet, Mr. Hudson. So despite what my sister Everly said, I'm not interested in being neighborly. Sorry if that hurts your big, fat ego, but count me out of any neighborhood barbecues."

Ian's hard gaze shifted. His dark glower was gone, and the ice faded from his eyes. Then his mouth turned up at the corners, making his entire expression change. Brandy could admit that her brutish neighbor was handsome in a hunk-of-a-man way, but Ian Hudson smiling made something deep inside her chest heat up.

"Perfect, Ms. Kane." Ian stepped away from the counter. "You won't have to worry about being neighborly, because the entire reason I live on acres of land by myself is because I want quiet, too."

Triumph zinged through Brandy. "Well, then, I guess we agree. Again, thanks for your help, and I'd say, 'See you around,' but I hope that doesn't happen."

Ian's smile spread.

That smile could weaken a woman's knees. Not Brandy's, of course. Handsome men were on Brandy's *completely ignore* list. Her heart had been shattered in so many pieces that she didn't even know where those pieces had ended up.

Ian's low voice rumbled in the silence between them. "Have a good, uh, week, Ms. Kane."

"You, too, Mr. Hudson."

She watched him turn and walk out of the cottage, which had seemed to shrink with him inside of it. Her breath escaped as the screen door banged behind him and his boots pounded across the porch. She heard a short conversation between the men, then Everly's voice piped up. Whatever they said, Ian Hudson disappeared moments later—back into the woods where he'd come from.

Finally.

Now, Brandy had to convince her sister and almost brother-in-law that she was fine. Bush cutting and porch sweeping could be done another day. Right now, she wanted to arrange her kitchen, make some orange tea, and watch the sun set on her first evening of her new life.

Heading out onto the porch, Brandy paused to see Everly and Austin *not* working, but standing together in an embrace, as if they'd just been kissing.

"Oh sorry, did I interrupt?" Brandy teased.

Everly looked over, her face flushed, but she made no effort to release Austin. "Not interrupting. Sorry, we'll get back to work and—"

"That's the thing," Brandy jumped in. "I think we've done enough hard labor for the day. I want to slow things down for the rest of the day. Tomorrow will come soon enough."

Everly laughed. "You mean Mom will show up?"

"Yep," Brandy said. "I need a quiet night before the storm hits."

Austin chuckled, then he released Everly. They were a striking couple—Austin with his dark hair and warm brown eyes, and Everly's honey-blonde hair and dancing hazel eyes. Her exuberant personality was a nice contrast to Austin's more serious nature.

Austin turned toward Brandy. "We've got a couple of hours to spare. My daughter is perfectly fine at her friend's house. Give us the hardest jobs."

Brandy held up her hand. "No, you're off the hook. You've done so much already. Really. Thank you so much."

"I get it," Everly said simply. She joined Brandy on the porch and hugged her. "You want some of that peace and quiet you've been craving since your return."

Brandy hugged her sister back. Since the big breakup with

Brock and the cancelation of her wedding one week before the big day, she'd taken a work hiatus and spent a couple of weeks at the beach in a town several hours away. When she'd finished nursing her deepest wounds, she let her mom and sister talk her into coming back to Everly Falls.

She'd moved back into her mom's house because that's where she'd been living while engaged to Brock. But the memories around town were too painful. The café where they'd eaten together, the bakery that had been making her wedding cake, the park where they'd taken long walks in the evening... And Brock himself still lived in Everly Falls.

She'd blocked his number, of course, but when she saw him in line at Marshall's Coffee early one morning, she knew she couldn't live in town anymore. Thus, the solution of relocating to Grandpa Miller's cottage—which Mom objected to. If anyone would understand, Everly would, since she'd dated Brock first.

Yeah... it was a mess.

Brandy was a mess. And she was tired of it. She was going to find her way through it all, though. All she needed was time and quiet and peace, and no nosy neighbors or people staring at her or asking her friendly but intrusive questions.

She didn't need the small town of Everly Falls to watch her faltering her way back to normal. Or *new* normal, she guessed.

"Thanks, sis," Brandy said, releasing Everly. "Seriously, I don't know what I'd do without you."

"Call me with anything you need." Everly drew her cell phone out of her pocket. "I have service, do you?"

Brandy checked her phone. "Yep. It's all good. And I'll be setting up my hot spot tonight, so things will be running smoothly."

"Still." Everly's brow dipped. "If things don't work out

here, I can talk to Darla about my old apartment. She's just using it for storage."

"I'll let you know." They'd been over this, though. The makeshift apartment over the craft store where Everly worked wasn't a better solution since it would put her right in the center of town. "Thanks again. Drive safe, and give Jessica a hug for me."

Jessica, Austin's seven-year-old daughter, had wrapped the entire Kane family around her finger. How would it be to be a kid again, with your whole life ahead of you, unaware of two-timing men and broken hearts?

**Heather B. Moore** is a *USA Today* bestselling author of more than ninety publications. Heather writes primarily historical and #herstory fiction about the humanity and heroism of the everyday person. Publishing in a breadth of genres, Heather dives into the hearts and souls of her characters, meshing her love of research with her love of storytelling.

Her biblical fiction and thrillers are written under pen name H.B. Moore. She writes historical women's fiction, romance, and inspirational non-fiction under Heather B. Moore, and . . . speculative fiction under Jane Redd. This can all be confusing, so her kids just call her Mom. Heather attended Cairo American College in Egypt and the Anglican School of Jerusalem in Israel. Despite failing her high school AP English exam, Heather persevered and earned a Bachelor of Science degree from Brigham Young University in something other than English.

For book updates, sign up for Heather's email list:
hbmoore.com/contact
Website: HBMoore.com
Instagram: @authorhbmoore

Facebook: Heather B. Moore All About Books
Blog: MyWritersLair.blogspot.com
Pinterest: @HeatherBMoore
TikTok: @heatherbmooreauthor
X: @HeatherBMoore
Threads: @AuthorHBMoore

www.ingramcontent.com/pod-product-compliance
Lightning Source LLC
LaVergne TN
LVHW021809060526
838201LV00058B/3293